THE DUKE'S PURSUIT

THE DUKE'S PURSUIT

GOLDEN ANGEL

CLEIS
PRESS

Published in the United States by Cleis Press, an imprint of Start Midnight, LLC, 221 River Street, Ninth Floor, Hoboken, New Jersey 07030.

Printed in the United States
Cover design: Jennfier Do
Cover image: Shutterstock
Text design: Frank Wiedemann
First Edition.
10 9 8 7 6 5 4 3 2 1

Trade paper ISBN: 978-1-62778-317-0
E-book ISBN: 978-1-62778-531-0

CHAPTER ONE

PHILIPPA CAPELL, DOWAGER COUNTESS OF
Essex, had decided to take a lover.

Her late husband, whose rakish nature had been undi-
minished by marriage, had enjoyed teaching her about
bedroom sport. She found, after a year and a half of
mourning, that while she might not have any interest in
love, her body still had an interest in those activities.

Unfortunately, she did not find them as pleasurable on
her own, and so she required a partner.

After all, she certainly had not planned on becoming
a widow at the young age of twenty and two. There were
some ladies of the same age present this evening who were
still engaged in the marriage mart, and here she was with
one husband already come and gone. Her late husband,
Clarence, had only been forty-seven when he'd been
thrown from his horse on a night ride into London to see
his mistress.

They had been married for only seven months at the
time.

Clarence had been introduced to her during her first
Season and had determined that Philippa, with her size-

able dowry, would make him an ideal second wife. That her father was a tradesman did not bother him—unlike some of the *ton*. Her father had been all too happy to accept the proposal, thrilled that she had caught the attention of an earl.

At the time she had been heartbroken from her first misadventure in love and eager to accept any arrangement that would allow her to retreat from London. A loveless marriage had sounded ideal. Clarence had been much older than her, of course, but he had treated her well enough, even if her dowry had been what interested him initially.

Marriage without love was preferable to putting herself in the position of heartbreak for a second time.

Once married, she'd learned that her new husband was a bit of a rake, and his knowledge of how to pleasure a woman had certainly distracted her from her broken heart. They'd had light friendship rather than love between them, but it was all Philippa had wanted. Especially since Clarence let her retire to his country estate, rather than having to face another moment of London Society and *him*.

Him being the man who had broken her heart before Clarence's proposal. Philippa did not even like to think *his* name anymore. Before his betrayal, she would have fought tooth and nail against Clarence's proposal. After it, she had eagerly taken the first chance to flee London and *him*. That her marriage also gave her a title, filling the lack *his* mother had found with Philippa, had been a small balm.

Staying in London had not been an option. She would have rather died than finish the Season watching *him* court and marry another woman, a woman whom his mother approved of.

For a mere six months, she had lived a quiet life as Clarence's countess at his country estate. Her new husband had enjoyed teaching her the joys of the marriage bed, and Philippa's heart had slowly healed. Not entirely. How could it, when Clarence found her wanting as well? He had tried to hide his mistresses from her, but Philippa had found the perfumed notes they sent him while he was away from town.

She had been confused more than angered, but Clarence had balked at attempting to explain why he still had a need for other women. As far as he was concerned, the topic was forbidden. It had not helped her confidence, and yet, strangely, it had not damaged their friendship either.

They had been at Clarence's country estate when one of his mistresses had called him back to London and he had gone in the dark. Philippa still did not know why the haste had been so necessary, but it had cost him his life. While she did not much miss his company during her days, as they had not spent much real time together, she did miss his presence at night in her bed and the pleasures that she had found there. She had been fond of Clarence and truly did mourn his loss.

After a year and a half of mourning and thinking, she had decided that she did not want to impose on her stepson Arthur any longer. Strange to think that she had a stepson who was three years older than her and newly married. He and Minerva deserved their time together, so when Olivia had written to her, begging her to come to London, Philippa had decided it was time. Her friend needed her, for it was Olivia's first Season since *her* scandalous marriage last year.

She could lend her moral support for Olivia and Francis, end her formal mourning, and engage in *amour.*

She was not interested in marrying again, but she missed the pleasures of the flesh. During her two Seasons before her own wedding, she had learned enough to know she would hardly be the only widow to behave in such a manner—although she might be the youngest. Indeed, the *ton* was flush with widows, and even some married ladies, who took lovers without scandal (or a minimal amount of scandal) as long as they were discreet. While Clarence had kept Philippa well satisfied in their bed, he had sometimes hinted at activities beyond those they engaged in, rousing her curiosity, which was something he had never satisfied, as he'd insisted that those activities were not suited to wives. Well, Philippa was no longer a wife, and she wanted to find out more about those mysterious acts that had kept Clarence visiting his mistresses.

Now, looking over the throngs of Society crowding Lady Jersey's ballroom, she wondered how one went about choosing and procuring a lover. Clarence had claimed that not all men concerned themselves with a lady's pleasure . . . but how was one to know if a man did or did not?

"Do you see anyone you're interested in, Pippa?" whispered Olivia excitedly, leaning in closer and covering her mouth with her fan. Her eyes danced with enthusiasm. "Ooo, what about him? He looks like a rake. Rakes must be good lovers, don't you think?"

Philippa was still not sure that telling her friend of her plan had been the wisest of decisions, but her enthusiasm could not be denied. And Philippa did need help, as well as a friend to confide in—and someone to pull on the reins if she witnessed Philippa becoming too involved. She had decided not to risk her heart in these ventures; indeed, she preferred to spread her favors among more than one gentleman.

After all, that was what Clarence had done with his women, leaving her to conclude that different lovers would offer different experiences. It seemed a sensible theory. And it would keep her from falling in too deeply with any one man in particular. She had learned that lesson. But she refused to think about *him*, although if he were in London then of course he would be here tonight. Everyone who was anyone would be; Lady Jersey's ball was the premiere event to begin the Season. Already the crush of people in the house was somewhat stifling.

"Shhh," she hushed her friend, lowering her tones even further than Olivia had. It would not do for anyone to overhear them. Especially Olivia's husband, who'd had a reputation for being almost too reputable before he had married Olivia. The marquess was walking with another friend behind them, and he probably could not hear them over the babbling of the crowd around them, but she did not want to take any chances. "I'm still looking."

"Perhaps you should stop looking and start dancing," Olivia whispered back. "If we stopped walking then perhaps someone might ask you to dance. You're looking particularly fine tonight, the gentlemen have been staring the entire turn we've done around the room."

Philippa blushed at her friend's compliment, for the first time paying attention to where the men were gazing rather than inspecting them for herself. Indeed, Olivia was correct. Several men were looking over at her. Some she recognized from her time as a debutante, and some were men that she had never been introduced to in order to protect her reputation. Although she was as young as some of the debutantes, albeit the older ones, she was dressed in a sapphire silk gown, a color that a debutante would never be allowed to wear, with a décolletage that would have been far too low for an unmarried virgin.

"Do you really think they're interested?" she whispered back. That had been her second greatest fear—to return to Society in search of expanding her bedroom education and finding that she was undesirable. Part of her had worried that perhaps Clarence had not found her quite desirable enough, and that it wasn't the lack of indecent activities with her that left him unsatisfied, but perhaps it was something about her personally. After all, she'd already had one experience of not being enough to secure a man's faithfulness. No. She wasn't going to think about *him* right now.

Olivia rolled her eyes.

"Of course. Not only are you even more beautiful than you were when you were first presented, for which I quite hate you, but that dress shows you off to perfection. Plus, you must admit, the two of us together make quite a striking pair." That was certainly true, and something that the two of them had taken advantage of. They set each other off wonderfully. Olivia and her sisters had hair so pale it was almost white, and Olivia's eyes were a deep, warm brown, whereas Philippa had dark brown hair and startling blue eyes. They complemented each other, especially tonight, with Olivia dressed in a gown made of honey-colored silk with amber edging and Philippa in her blue, which made her eyes glow like jewels.

In fact, it appeared they did not actually need to stop their amble around the room in order to attract a gentleman—they merely needed to look up.

"Lady Hertford," said a young gentleman, stepping rather brazenly in their path. Philippa looked at him curiously, as he was not a gentleman that she recognized from her two prior Seasons, although he must have been around at the time since he only seemed to be a few years older than herself. Very handsome, with the lazy smile of a born rake, and blond hair that was rather attractively combed to highlight his dark brown eyes. It was an arresting combination, very nearly the opposite of her own. He cut a rather dashing figure clad in black and gold, with a deep burgundy waistcoat to give him a bit of color.

"Lord Sunderland," Olivia intoned politely, although Philippa could tell from the edge in her friend's voice that she wasn't entirely pleased by this introduction. She conjectured from Lord Sunderland's attire and demeanor that he must not be entirely reputable, although obviously powerful enough that Olivia could not give him a direct cut either. Earl of Sunderland . . . that would make him . . . oh good heavens! The grandson of the Duke of Marlborough, which meant that this young man stood to inherit a very rich and powerful position after his grandfather and father passed. No wonder Olivia did not cut him, despite his rakish demeanor and his brazen inspection of their attire. "I did not know you were in London."

"First Season in years." He smiled and winked at her. "It feels odd to see you here rather than at one of the country fetes, does it not?"

"Sunderland." Francis suddenly appeared at his wife's elbow, as if drawn by the presence of a practiced seducer.

It would have been amusing if it weren't so touching to see his protectiveness. Olivia swore it wasn't a love match, that Francis had merely married her to save her reputation, but Philippa thought her friend might be a bit blind to her husband's regard. "How are you enjoying your evening?"

"Quite well, although I daresay my evening would improve dramatically if you would introduce me to this delightful beauty," he said, turning the full force of his dark eyes on Philippa. She could not help but feel her lips curving into a smile, even as she recognized that he was going to be nothing more than a flirt. As if she had not already had her fill of those in her life. But since she was looking for experienced men to share amorous affairs with, then surely she need look no further than the rather attractive man in front of her!

Olivia gave her a significant glance as she slid her arm away, putting some distance between them so that Philippa might offer Lord Sunderland her hand. "Lord Sunderland, this is my dear friend Philippa Capell, the Dowager Countess of Essex. Lady Essex, this is Felix Churchill, the Earl of Sunderland."

"My lord," Philippa murmured as he kissed the back of her glove. "I am pleased to make your acquaintance."

"Not as pleased as I am," he said with a wink, holding her hand for just a moment too long. Then he grinned, delighted, as she laughed at his outrageous flirtations. "Might I claim a dance?"

"I believe I have an immediate opening on my card," she said, placing her hand back in his as he held it out. With a smile to Olivia, Philippa let the dashing Lord Sunderland lead her to the dance floor for a quadrille.

Not surprisingly, he was a very good dancer, although

his hand did tend to linger in hers longer than propriety called for. Still, she enjoyed herself, well aware that she was displaying herself to her advantage as her skirts swayed in time with the music. They chatted lightly after he offered his condolences on the loss of her husband, as well as his joy that she had come out of mourning, for such a beauty belonged in London where she could be properly appreciated. Although Philippa was quite confident in her looks, she found that she still enjoyed the many compliments that Lord Sunderland rained down upon her.

The strange thing was, despite the numerous accolades he heaped upon her, his demeanor was not that of a seducer. While she felt his interest keenly, there was something slightly off about it. As if he was interested in her, but not in a romantic way.

It was decidedly odd.

At the end of the dance Lord Sunderland returned her to Olivia, who was chatting with her younger sister's good friend Charlotte Greville. The daughter of the Earl of Warrick, Miss Greville was in her third Season and was still on the hunt for a well-off husband, preferably with a more noble title than her father's. The earl was well known for his scandalously expensive habits, which included both gambling and women, and Charlotte wanted a better life than the one she was currently living. As such, Charlotte had made herself one of the Originals of the Season, with her dark red hair and glowing green eyes. She was wearing a green gown that was several shades brighter than the pastels a debutante normally wore. It certainly made the most of her eyes, which she batted prettily at the earl, obviously well informed as to his future titles. He might not be a duke anytime soon, but he would be after his grandfather and father, and that made him quite a catch for Miss Greville.

Unfortunately for her, the lord immediately begged off, claiming to need some fresh air from the gardens.

"Of course, my lord," Charlotte said, adding boldly, "I would be happy to hold a later dance open for you."

"And I would be delighted to add my name to your card," Lord Sunderland said smoothly, although Philippa thought that his tone was a bit too stilted to be genuine. However, he had wonderful manners, and he added his name to the dance card hanging from Charlotte's wrist before giving the three ladies a bow and taking himself off.

"That was rather bold," Olivia said, scolding Charlotte as soon as Lord Sunderland was out of earshot. "You don't want him to think you're fast, do you? Heavens knows what your mother will say when she finds out I've allowed Sunderland to secure a dance with you."

"Mama won't mind," Charlotte said absently, her gaze following Sunderland's progress from the ballroom. "His reputation notwithstanding, he's hasn't been about in London in *years*, and he's still the heir to a dukedom. She'd have had a fit if I'd let him get away without securing a dance. Besides, Philippa danced with him."

"Philippa doesn't have to worry about her reputation the way you do," Olivia said rather severely. "She's been married already, and her virtue was assured before her wedding."

"And he asked me to dance, not the other way round," Philippa said helpfully. Poor Olivia, Lady Warrick must have left Charlotte in her care while the countess went to the card tables in the other room, as she was wont to do. Chaperoning someone like Charlotte, who seemed ready to ruin herself in a moment if it would get her the financial stability that she craved, would grate on anyone's nerves.

The redhead proved her temperament by glaring at Philippa in a most unladylike manner. "Well, some of us need a husband more than others."

"Charlotte!" admonished Olivia while Philippa winced at the crude, but unfortunately accurate, accusation. "You'll be lucky if you land a husband at all with that shrewish tongue. Jealousy is unbecoming. So is boldness."

The younger girl rolled her eyes. "You were bold enough once, Olivia. Otherwise you would not have married the way you did."

"No, I was inordinately lucky, or I would not have married the way I did," Olivia said tightly. "Obviously my sister Alice has not told you the entire story if you think that I was bold. And I won't be repeating it here. Needless to say, I would not count on having my kind of lucky intervention should you be so unlucky as to fall into a similar situation."

Looking rather surprised at Olivia's grim tones, Charlotte deflated a little. Especially as another gentleman approached, his eyes on Philippa.

"My dear Lady Essex, how good to see you back in Society," said the Duke of Beaufort, bowing over her hand. In his forties, the bachelor duke still cut a regal and handsome figure. With his short, cropped sandy blond hair, which had a few glints of silver in it, not to mention his position in Society, he was the cause for many sighs amongst the ladies. Every Season, women set their cap for him, hoping that this would be the Season he'd finally take a wife to get his heir, and every Season he disappointed them. He had been quite good friends with her late husband Clarence, and so Philippa had cause to know that his lack of interest in a wife stemmed from his great love for his mistress, Helena, whom Philippa had heard of when the men were in the cups.

"It is wonderful to be here, your grace," Philippa said, curling her fingers around his hand. "May I introduce my dear friend Olivia Seymour, the Marchioness of Hertford, and our friend Charlotte Greville."

"Ladies," said the duke politely. "I hope you don't mind, but I'd like to steal Lady Essex away for a dance."

"Of course," Olivia said graciously as Charlotte pouted. Philippa turned to lead Curtis away before he could see the unbecoming reaction. Not that she thought Charlotte would make a good wife for him, but she knew that Curtis wouldn't hesitate to come down on her for such behavior. Unlike the majority of the *ton*, he was actually in a position where he could do so, being good friends with her father.

"You're looking more beautiful than ever, Lady Essex," the duke said as he led her back to the dance floor, where they were playing a waltz. Thank heavens she'd be doing this with Curtis; this would be her first waltz back in Society, and she would not have been comfortable dancing it with someone she did not know.

"Please, your grace, I know I've asked you to call me Philippa before," she protested, now that they were having a private conversation.

"Well then none of this 'your grace' nonsense from you," he retorted.

"Of course, Curtis," she said with a smile as he swept her up into his arms.

"Are you sure you don't mind?" he asked. "With Clarence gone, I thought perhaps a return to formality might be more appropriate."

"Absolutely not," she said firmly as they began to move around the floor, feeling strangely aware of his hand on her back and the closeness of his body. It had been so long since she'd waltzed that she'd forgotten how close and intimate a dance it could be. "You were my friend as well as his, after all. At least, I hope so," she added with her eyes twinkling.

Curtis chuckled. "I do count you amongst my friends, Philippa. A very good one, in fact."

"Here he comes!" announced Michael Conyngham from his spot as lookout in the gardens. It had been a long ten minutes as they'd waited for Felix's return from the ballroom so that they could set their wager.

The small group of young men gathered in the gardens cheered the news, clustering around the two men at the heart of the wager: Everett Cavendish, the Marquess of Hartington and one day to be the Duke of Devonshire, and Rupert Conyngham, the Earl of Conyngham and one day its Marquess. Although good friends, the two rogues had a two-year-long rivalry over which of them was the more talented seducer, usually culminating in some kind of wager that must be met over the Season. Last year Conyngham had sworn retaliation after Hartington managed to steal a kiss from the Season's most celebrated new debutante.

They were well matched, as Rupert was only a year younger than Everett's twenty-eight years, although Everett obviously had the advantage when it came to titles. However, Conyngham tended to have fewer scruples than Hartington, especially when it came to debutantes. He also frequented the bawdy houses, whereas Everett confined his interests to widows and unhappy wives. Rupert had been known to jest that Everett only made do with two of the three W's—widows, wives, and whores!

When it came to looks, they each collected sighs from the ladies, and for vastly different reasons. Rupert Conyngham was almost boyishly good-looking, with a kind of innocence to his face that had women comparing him to an angel on a regular basis. With his sun-kissed brown hair, ever-changing hazel eyes, athletically lean body, and winning smile, it was no wonder that he managed to charm his way out of situations that would destroy another man.

For a certainty, Everett thought ruefully, he would not have been able to talk his way out of some of the situations that Conyngham had successfully wriggled free from. Standing taller than any of his friends, with a set of shoulders to match, he could not look anything but authoritative. The striking combination of jet-black hair and emerald green eyes, and the surprising dimples that flashed when he smiled, endeared him to the feminine sex as much as his striking figure.

Indeed, Conyngham and Hartington were considered a jolly good match when it came to wagers involving ladies, for they each had their own particular set of skills and advantages.

This Season's lark should prove highly entertaining, as the young men had been deciding on the guidelines for several months now. At Lady Jersey's ball a neutral party would select a lady, either married or widowed, before any of their group circulated through the ballroom. Then the lady would be pointed out to the group, and Conyngham and Hartington would both vie for her attention, the first to seduce her obviously being the winner. Wagers had been laid down blind on both sides, as well as several side bets having to do with timing, location, and the other particulars on which young gentlemen enjoyed wagering.

Lord Felix Churchill, the Earl of Sunderland, had been assigned the part of selecting a lady. His father had kept him cooped up at their home in the country learning how to run the estates and instilling a strong sense of duty in him for the past few years, and so he was unfamiliar with the London crowd, and therefore agreed upon as the best neutral judge. Having been inured from the gossip that permeated every Season, he would choose based on beauty and deportment alone.

When he reached the head of the stairs that led down into the gardens, he waved at them, indicating that they should join him up on the patio, which they hastened to do so. As he led them into the hall overlooking the ballroom he was practically crowing with delight. Conyngham and Hartington stood on either side of him, looking down at the many guests that were dancing around the floor. Being a story above the crowd gave them the advantage of having a conversation unobserved, as well as a bird's-eye view of the gentlemen and ladies.

"She perfect," Felix was practically babbling. "A widow, newly arrived, and a complete nonpareil in beauty. It'll be a fit competition, there's no doubt she'll have other suitors."

"Perhaps I'll end up putting my money on one of them," Michael joked, grinning unabashedly when his brother sent him a quelling look.

"Only if you're planning on losing it," Rupert retorted, nudging Michael in the side at the show of disloyalty. Everett ignored them both as Roger Hervey, the second son of the Earl of Jermyn and his best friend, joined him at the balcony. While Roger was known as being a bit of a rake, he was also disapproving of Everett's friendly rivalry with Rupert, feeling that such blatant competition did a disservice to both of them.

"It's not too late to back out," Roger murmured into Everett's ear. Being just an inch shorter than Everett's impressive height, he was one of few men able to do so easily. "This kind of wager could go very badly for everyone involved."

"It will be fine," Everett said, still amused by his friend's show of priggishness. Roger had been set against this wager from the beginning, considering it demeaning and potentially ruinous to a lady's reputation. But that was why Felix had chosen a widow after all. An experienced lady who had cast off her mourning and whose reputation wouldn't be damaged when two rogues began to court her. In fact, it was quite possible that her reputation would be enhanced, albeit in a slightly scandalous way.

"Ah-ha! There she is!" said the excited Felix, having finally spotted her amidst the crush. "In the blue gown, dancing with the Duke of Beaufort."

Beaufort was holding her rather closely, Everett was amused to notice. He'd heard the duke was wife-hunting this Season, hoping to find an indulgent woman who wouldn't mind him keeping the long-term mistress who held his heart. Was he hoping that this widow might be so inclined? Considering his fortune and title, it shouldn't be too hard for the man to find such a wife, but perhaps he was looking for some kind of true companionship as well. Looking down at the woman who was dancing with Beaufort, he admired the creaminess of her skin, displayed to advantage by the low cut of the gown.

She was quite beautiful, from the glimpses he could catch as Beaufort whirled her around the floor. Felix was babbling about her conversation and deportment as the men watched her. Even Roger was leaning forward, as if he wanted a better look at her. Younger than Everett had expected, with the most extraordinarily dark hair, it almost put him in mind of . . .

Her face tipped back in a laugh, and his heart stuttered to a stop as Felix answered Conyngham's question. "Her name? Lady Philippa Capell."

Through the roaring in his ears he heard Roger's gasp, indicating that his friend recognized this travesty as well.

Pippa.

CHAPTER TWO

THE FIRST TIME EVERETT SAW PIPPA WAS IN a ballroom just like this, only it was the beginning of her first Season as a debutante and she'd just been presented. He'd been struck by her nearly black hair and clear blue eyes; she was the only other person besides him that he had ever met to have black hair and light eyes. They'd been drawn to each other immediately, and he'd created quite the scandal that evening by dancing with her twice and barely leaving her side. It had not taken him long to discover that she was more than just a beautiful face, although she was certainly one of those. That Season men had swarmed to court her and Olivia, Lady Twilight and Lady Dawn they called them.

However, he was quite sure that he was the only one who had been lucky enough to discover the real Pippa. Not the well-mannered miss that most of the world saw. They scoured bookstores together so that he could purchase loftier works for her than would normally be sold to a young miss, watched lowbrow theater and street performers in Covent Garden, and one evening snuck out to watch a star shower. While she presented a face of complete propriety to the rest of the world, easily done as she excelled at singing, the pianoforte, watercolors, and embroidery, Everett was privileged to hear her thoughts and fears, her dreams and plans. They'd fallen head over heels in love, and he'd gone from being a young gentleman whose behavior was occasionally rakish to an upstanding young man considering marriage.

Unfortunately, his parents were horrified by his choice in bride.

A future duke does *not* marry the daughter of a tradesman, no matter how wealthy. His mother went into fits of vapors that some title-hunting chit had duped her son. His father suggested offering her carte blanche and making her his mistress. Everett had stormed out in furious despair after his father threatened to cut him off completely, deny him any kind of housing or allowance if he married her. Marrying her would dishonor his family's name, his father insisted, and destroy his mother. He would do anything to keep that from happening, even force Everett to dishonor himself further by working as a regular tradesman.

Torn between duty and love, he'd gone to Pippa and told her that he needed some time to think. He'd explained the situation and she'd pushed him, not caring that they might have to work to support themselves. She was certain that his parents would come around eventually, once they realized that she wasn't hunting for a title or wealth, that she only wanted him. She was sure they could be happy. Everett had told her that she did not understand, could not possibly understand, because she wasn't nobility.

That's what he told himself, too. It was only later that he realized how fear had made him lie to himself.

Their discussion had ended in a furious fight, and she'd refused to back down, declaring that she'd wait for him—but not forever. It had stung his pride, hurt his heart that she'd threatened him, as he saw it. Then he'd made the stupidest decision of his life.

He'd purposefully had her catch him, not two evenings later, kissing Lady Alice Dormer in the garden. Roger had been the one to fetch her outside so that she could see Everett entwined with the lady. Some immature, idiotic part of him had wanted to show her that she was not the only one with other options. He'd wanted to spurn her, break her heart, before she had the opportunity to break his. The devastation he'd seen on her face had splintered his own heart into pieces. The very next day, he'd run away to the country, needing space from London, the bloody Season, and his parents. He'd stayed there a month, gathering his courage to defy his parents, but by the time he returned, it was too late.

Roger was the one to inform him that Pippa had practically disappeared from the Season at the same time he had. Spreading gossip said that he had ruined her and run. Before it could spread too far, her father had married her off to the Earl of Essex, Clarence Capell, and the gossip had died down. Turned, actually—now they were saying that she had spurned his suit and caused him to run off to rusticate. The earl had removed himself and his new bride off to his country seat, and Everett spent the rest of the Season running rampant. There were plenty of women, wives and widows, ready to comfort him. He indulged in women, drink, and gambling, furious at his parents and determined to show them exactly what their snobbery, vapors, and threats had cost them.

GOLDEN ANGEL

Since then, he'd joined the crowd around Rupert
Conyngham, now known as Rupert's Rakes to the
gossip-hungry *ton*, and his parents despaired of him
ever marrying. Everett had not danced with a debutante
since Pippa. He had not *loved* a woman since Pippa. He'd
despaired when she had not returned to London after her
husband unexpectedly passed . . .

But she was here now.

Roger's hand gripped Everett's upper arm hard, his
fingers digging in tightly enough to bruise his flesh,
bringing Everett back to the present. "You can't do this,"
Roger hissed. "You'd have to be insane."

"Can't I?" asked Everett. "Of course, I can."

"He can if he wants to," said Rupert from the other
side of Felix, still watching Pippa as she finished dancing
with the duke. "I certainly am."

All their friends knew that Everett had quarreled with
his parents about his lack of interest in marrying, none
but Roger knew the reason why. They were the cause
of gossip, they did not listen to it, and so they had no
idea about the history between Everett and the Dowager
Countess of Essex.

Everett could not take his eyes off her. She was stunning, even more beautiful than she'd been three years ago.
If she'd been a diamond in the rough then, now she was
a flawless gem, cut and polished by her life to shine ever
brighter.

"You can't possibly think this is a good idea," Roger
said, his voice low in Everett's ear, the grip of his fingers
unrelenting. "Do you remember what it was like the last
time she broke your heart? Do you?"

"I broke hers first," Everett murmured so that only

Roger would hear him. Yes, he remembered those black days. Sort of, anyway. He'd spent a lot of them drunk or recovering from too much drinking. Even tried opium once, before Roger had dragged him out of the den and threatened to beat him if he ever did that again. Poor Roger. No wonder he was worried.

After all, he'd been the one to pick Everett up and dust him off over and over again during those dark days. He'd been the one to listen to hours of maudlin ruminations and brokenhearted declarations, to put off the duke and duchess when Everett wasn't fit for company, and to eventually drag Everett into some semblance of living again. Even if it was living as a rake. That was Everett's decision after all, and loyal Roger had followed him into the lifestyle, even though Roger did not make much of a rogue.

"What will your father say?"

"Bugger my father. He might even be happy to see me settle down, whatever the lady's pedigree. Even if he's not, I don't give a damn anymore."

Roger gaped at him, his blue eyes filled with shock.

"You mean to marry her?"

"I won't let her get away from me again Roger. I can't."

This was his second chance, a chance that he'd never thought he'd get. When he'd heard about her husband's passing, he'd almost ridden out to see her immediately, but had realized how inappropriate such an action would be while she was in mourning. And he'd had no idea how he'd be received. When she'd stayed away from London after her year of mourning was over, he'd realized that she must not want to see him at all and that she was avoiding Society, which broke his heart all over again. But he'd respected her space and had not written or gone to her as he'd yearned to.

Now she had returned. One way or another, he would make her his again, and this time he would not be stupid enough to let her go.

"Look, she's talking to Cal's sister. We can use him to gain an introduction," Rupert said, moving immediately. Calvin followed him obligingly until Rupert turned, realizing that Everett wasn't following him. "Aren't you coming Hartington? Or do you cede the field already?"

"Don't worry about me, Conyngham. I'll garner my own introduction," Everett said with a smile, leaning against the balcony with a casualness that he did not feel. Of course men were going to flock to Pippa, they had before, after all. And now she was a widow out of mourning and there was no longer any need to dance around her virtue; as long as everyone was discreet then there would be no repercussions. But he'd held her affections once before, and he was certain he could again. This was simply not the time or place to reintroduce himself.

Before losing Pippa he had been, if not the perfect son, a very good son to his parents. A man about town rather than a rake, charming, well-mannered, and only a little fast. He'd bowed to their snobbery and the demands that he cease his pursuit of Pippa, although at the time he had not meant to cut her off altogether. Just to slow things down until he could determine the best route to pleasing both his parents and himself. Instead, Philippa had married someone else, and it was only when she was truly lost to him that he had realized how badly he'd allowed his parents to affect his life.

Everett's descent into life as a rake had begun not only because he'd lost Pippa, but because of his depression and anger over his own inability to withstand his parents' censure. Since that time, he'd become quite practiced at not caring about their opinion and doing what pleased him. Not that he became an entirely selfish creature, but he found that he cared quite a bit less for his supposed prestige and reputation than he'd originally thought. Unfortunately, none of that could bring Philippa back to him.

He considered this second chance nothing less than divine intervention.

Shrugging at his friend's folly, the Earl of Conyngham followed Calvin down to the first floor and the merry widow.

As Philippa was led off the floor by his grace, she saw Francis leading Olivia out to dance. Smiling at her friend's obvious happiness in her marriage, she excused herself from the duke so that she could wend her way through the crowd to her friend Juliet Parker, who had finally arrived. Against a delightful dress of apricot silk, Juliet's auburn hair looked even more reddish, and her hazel eyes were glinting with mischief as she saw Philippa approaching.

"Pipp— I mean, Philippa, darling," Juliet quickly corrected herself. She'd almost used the old nickname that Philippa could not bear to hear anymore. Not since *him*. "Olivia told me you were back this Season! You look absolutely lovely. I cannot wait until I can wear something other than these insipid pastels."

Philippa laughed as they clasped each other's hands, hurrying over to a bench where they could sit and catch up. So far as she could tell, Juliet had not changed a bit.

They'd kept in contact through letters, but she had not seen her friend since her wedding.

"The fastest way out of the pastels is through a husband," Pippa teased as Juliet groaned.

"Don't remind me. At this rate I'll have to wait till I'm officially on the shelf before mother lets me wear anything with real color."

"Still on the quest for the perfect man? How many proposals have you turned down now?"

"Nine. Four my first Season, three my second, and two last Season," Juliet said, fanning herself delicately as her eyes roamed the room.

"Oh dear, so the numbers are going down?" Pippa laughed, knowing that the dwindling numbers wouldn't bother her friend in the slightest. Philippa was quite sure that the dwindling numbers were due more to Juliet's adeptness at indicating to suitors that she would not accept a proposal before one had even been made, rather than to a lack of desire.

"Down, up, it doesn't really matter until I find the right gentleman," Juliet said giggling, her spirits not at all dampened by the declining number.

"But what if the perfect man never sets himself forward because he's too frightened of being refused?"

"Then he's a ponce and not the perfect gentleman!"

"I say Juliet, language!" The cultured tones of a young gentleman caused them to turn, still laughing. Philippa immediately recognized Juliet's older brother and smiled, knowing the viscount was just as despairing of Juliet ever finding a husband as their father was. Of course, for Calvin it might be a more immediate worry, as he'd be the one charged with tending to a spinster sister. Not to mention that Olivia had told her he was running with a rather fast crowd; it must be awfully hard for him to keep his friends from ruining his sister.

"I say Calvin, bugger off," Juliet retorted, winking impishly at the handsome man standing beside Calvin. Despite the innocent boyishness of his face, the confident manner in which the man held himself told Philippa that he must be one of the "fast crowd" Calvin ran with. "Good evening, my lord," Juliet said, addressing the other man.

The sudden change in Juliet's voice from amused tolerance of her brother to utter flirtatiousness for "my lord" had Philippa turning to her friend in surprise. The sly smile Juliet sent her direction nearly caused Philippa to snort. The man in question must indeed be a rake for Juliet to pretend to flirt with him so blatantly. Calvin, meanwhile, seemed to be fuming a bit about the ears, and he glared rather heavily at his friend.

Deciding to stem the growing possibility of an incident, Philippa held out her hand to Juliet's brother, smiling sweetly. "Viscount Boringdon, it's delightful to see you again."

Being presented with a lady, Boringdon's manners kicked back in and he smiled at her as he took her hand and bowed over it, giving her a quick kiss on the back of her glove. The roguish grin he gave her had more than a small tinge of wickedness in it that made her blink. Good grief these siblings were a potent pair!

"Lady Essex, may I speak on behalf of all the gentlemen of London when I say your return is most welcome."

"I'd rather speak on my own behalf, if you don't mind," his friend said, nudging him in the side.

"Ah yes, my apologies. Lady Essex, this is my good friend the Earl of Conyngham. Conyngham, may I introduce you to Lady Essex."

"Charmed," Conyngham said as he stepped forward and quickly claimed her hand, his hazel eyes glinting with the same practiced wicked promise that Boringdon had shown. After kissing her hand, he held it, stepping even closer and forcing her to tilt her head back to look up at him. Quite a rogue! Philippa felt her heart pound a little faster at this blatant show of interest. "Please, dear Lady Essex, say that you still have a dance open on your card for me, or poor Calvin will have to spend the rest of the evening consoling me."

Philippa's eyes were sparkling with merriment at his flirtation. She felt quite sure that he must be at least a bit of a rake, and quite an attractive one too. The boyishness of his face made him seem almost innocent, but the way he spoke to her belied that illusion. Out of the corner of her eye she could see Juliet waving her fan, but then Calvin grabbed his sister's arm and began whispering in her ear. Consulting her card and ignoring the siblings, Philippa smiled up at the earl. "I do believe I have one opening left, my lord."

"Not anymore," he said, penciling his name in for the quadrille later this evening and completing her card. The triumph in his voice surprised her a little—she had not realized that he'd truly coveted a dance with her so much. Then again, if he was a rake, then he'd see dancing with a young widow as a gateway to other pleasures. At the moment, she was certainly finding herself amenable to such an idea. "Next time I hope you might save me waltz." He winked, and Philippa brought her fan up quickly to hide her smile at his audacity. He and Calvin bowed. "Ladies."

As the men walked away Juliet grabbed Philippa's arm, pulling her close to whisper in her ear. "Don't you know who that was?"

"He was introduced as the Earl of Conyngham, was he not?" Philippa asked, curious about her friend's behavior.

Suddenly Olivia popped up in front of them, looking all aflutter. Behind her stood Francis, scowling in Calvin and the earl's wake. "Oh my goodness, was that Conyngham over here? What did he want?"

"An introduction and a dance I believe," Philippa said calmly. Olivia's eyes got very wide and Francis turned his head back towards them, his scowl deepening.

"Don't tell me you said yes? Don't you know who he is?" Olivia asked, just as Francis spoke, over his wife: "You don't have to dance with him if you don't want to, I'll see to it."

"Good heavens," said Philippa, rather aghast at her friend's odd behavior. "Just who is he other than the Earl of Conyngham?"

"He's Rupert," said Juliet in tones of great significance.

"He's a scoundrel!" said Francis with great condemnation.

"He's friends with Everett," said Olivia, quite quietly.

All the breath seemed to go out of her lungs. No one had spoken *his* name in her presence in . . . well since before her wedding day. Francis was regarding his wife with some suspicion, obviously not understanding the significance of her revelation. Philippa pursed her lips to hide her reaction and seized on the less affecting nugget of information. "Rupert? You mean of Rupert's Rakes?"

"Yes, and unfortunately Calvin is one of those rakes," said Juliet, rolling her eyes. "They really aren't an entirely bad lot, but they can be quite wild, and I am sure the earl has the lowest of intentions when it comes to you. He's not a bad sort, quite amusing and dashing of course, like all rakes, but he does have a penchant for widows, and none at all for fidelity."

Which makes him different from most men? Philippa thought with a snort. She kept such thoughts to herself, because obviously Francis was made of different stuff. But he was an anomaly as far as she was concerned. Trust Olivia to find the one true man in England.

"I see," she said, and she flashed a dazzling smile at Francis. "Thank you for your support my lord, but I have no qualms about dancing with Lord Conyngham. I am sure he will behave himself in a ballroom, and as a widow to a former rake I have some experience in dealing with the breed."

"Of course," the marquess said with a slight bow, looking more at ease after the reminder that she was not a virginal debutante and that he need not worry over his wife's friend. "Do not hesitate to ask should you require my assistance."

"Thank you," she said gently, shooting Olivia an amused look. Francis really was a dear, but this just proved that he would certainly not understand that she had wanted to dance with Lord Conyngham specifically *because* he was a rake. Of course she would be discreet about her desires, and that meant not sullying his or Juliet's ears with her plans. Although Juliet would probably prove supportive if she did. And it seemed that her brother might be able to introduce her to any number of ah . . . experienced men.

Including *him*. The one she refused to name in her thoughts. Did Conyngham know of the connection? Would it bother him? Doubtful. If she had ever meant anything to *him* then he wouldn't have . . . never mind. The pain in her chest was almost overwhelming, even after all this time. If there were any vestiges of feeling in *him* for her, they would surely have to do with possession, not anything meaningful.

Just as she realized that her three friends were watching her in silence with varying degrees of consternation on their faces, Mr. Haverly came up to claim his dance with her. One of the younger sons of Baron Barnard, he was a pleasant-faced man in his early thirties. She had already danced with him once this evening and found him pleasant company; now she was even more grateful to him for rescuing her from a conversation that was rapidly becoming more awkward.

Unfortunately, their second dance wasn't quite as pleasant as their first; she found she was quite distracted by thoughts of Conyngham and *him*. Which was worse: if Conyngham knew of her connection to *him* and was interested in her in spite of it, or if he had no idea because *he* had never mentioned her to his friends? To be truthful, she wasn't sure which she preferred. Even more distracting was that once she thought she actually saw *him*, before she had to remind herself that every tall man with black hair was not necessarily *him*. It was just that her thoughts were tending towards him at the moment, and so naturally she might jump to that conclusion.

Despite her preoccupation with her thoughts, Mr. Haverly announced that she was a wonderful dancer and asked if he might call upon her the next day. Feeling soothed by his attention, Philippa informed him that she would be at home in the afternoon to receive callers. A few dances later she enjoyed the Earl of Conyngham's company, who was quite attentive in a very flattering manner, although she held herself back a bit from him, having not had the chance to work through her own feelings surrounding the information she'd received after meeting him. Her slight reticence only seemed to encourage him, and she found herself laughing at his salacious wit.

Twice more that evening she thought she might have glimpsed *him* through the crowd. She had to admit to herself that it was a possibility—after all, everyone who was anyone was here. And as a future duke, *he* was the very top of the "anyones," she thought bitterly. Finally, telling Olivia that she had a headache, Philippa made her escape.

Everett watched as his quarry climbed into her hansom and left. He was quite sure that she'd seen him at least once tonight, although he'd tried to stay out of her field of vision, wanting to watch her discreetly. Wondering if she'd changed. She was just as prim and proper as ever in front of the *ton*. None of them knew the girl that she was inside, except perhaps a few especial friends. Once he'd been numbered among them.

Part of him had wanted to approach her, but he dared not. He was too liable to do or say something stupid; after all, he'd had quite a shock just from discovering that she was in London, much less at Lady Jersey's ball. Considering their past, he needed to think out a plan. A better plan than taking every man she'd danced with tonight and throwing them in the Thames. Even if he did still like the sound of that plan.

"Are you sure you want to do this?" asked loyal Roger, the other reason Everett had managed the fortitude not to approach Pippa directly this evening. He was standing beside Everett, as he had been all night in worry over his friend, rather than paying any attention to the own lady of his desires. Roger was truly the best friend Everett had ever had, and he felt rather guilty that Roger's friendship had meant attending to Everett all night. He wouldn't take advantage of his friend like that again. Now that he knew Pippa was back, he would come up with a plan and stick to it, and Roger would be able to tend to his own affairs.

"Yes," he answered him with his usual cocky smile, although underneath it he was feeling quite anxious. "I was sure of her three years ago, but I allowed my parents to influence me. I should have married her then. I'm not going to let a second chance get away from me."

Lying in his lonely bed, sleep was proving to be elusive. Before tonight he had not thought of his bed as being lonely. If he wanted company for the night, it had always been easy to attain. But tonight, the only woman he could think about—the one he now realized he had been doing his best to forget by attempting to replace her with other women—was Pippa. The way she had looked this evening. The way she had moved. The way she had pulled at his emotions.

She'd grown even more beautiful, if that were possible. The sweet beauty of an innocent debutant had given way to a more mature elegance, a gracefulness and self-assurance that she had not possessed during her first Season. The changes were more than physical, and he had felt

33

drawn like a moth to a flame. She behaved like a woman with expectations, with experience. There was a sensuality to her that had not been there before.

Staring up at the ceiling, watching the light of the moon play with the shadows of his room, he felt a smile curve his lips. He had not thought of Pippa at night since her wedding day. It had always been too painful, knowing another man was gracing her bed, enjoying the delights of her body. He'd been wracked with jealousy and self-recrimination, and had done his best to erase those images from his mind by seducing other women and indulging in fleshly pleasures.

Now that she was a widow, free of the bonds of marriage and therefore available to him once more, the envy was easily tamped down. Everett was determined that Pippa would be the last lady he ever seduced, the final lady to grace his bed, and the only lady to be his wife. They would find the pleasure, love, and the happiness that had been denied to them her first Season. The happiness he had lost by giving in to his parents' pressure rather than claiming what he truly wanted.

Picturing her gracing *his* bed, her dark hair flowing across the crisp white pillow, he could imagine her completely undressed and ready for him. She would be cream and rose, with tightly budded nipples for him to kiss and suckle. He would finally hear her breathy gasps, her soft moans, as he used all the skills he'd acquired over the years to pleasure her. His cock rose as his imagination took wing, and he gripped the thick stalk, imagining it was her hand wrapping slender fingers around him. Her pouty lips hovering over his, her fingers stroking him.

"*I want you, Everett,*" she whispered in his mind, her voice sultry with arousal. He had almost forgotten the sound of her voice, but now it was clear in his mind again, beguiling him as easily as a siren. "*I need you inside me.*"

He would wrap his fingers around the back of her neck, pulling her down for a kiss. Tasting her. Enjoying her.

Groaning, Everett began to pump his cock.

When he seduced Pippa, he would take his time. Lavish kisses across her breasts, suckling her nipples until they were swollen and throbbing. He would worship every inch of her body, treating her like the goddess she was, making up for every second of lost time between them, rousing her to a fever pitch before thrusting inside of her and finally joining them together. She would be like silk around his cock, her muscles tensing and clenching, massaging the whole length as he rode her.

He would take her to the heights of ecstasy, show her everything they had not been able to explore together before . . . banish the thought of any other man from her mind. She would scream his name, quivering around him, flushed and hot and completely his.

His hips lifted, cock thrusting in his fist as he imagined Pippa writhing for him. Her cries filling his ear, her pleasure for him and him alone. Passion, ecstasy . . . love . . . The wet heat would spill over his groin and then his own climax would follow.

Gasping for breath, he slowed his strokes on his cock as hot liquid spurted, releasing the tension that had wracked his body.

In his mind's eye, Pippa smiled up at him, the lazy smile of a satisfied woman. A woman who loved him and was well-loved in return, happy to be his.

Sighing, he reluctantly opened his eyes, leaving his fantasy for the sticky reality that now coated his stomach. *Soon,* he promised himself silently. *Soon.*

CHAPTER THREE

THE MORNING AFTER LADY JERSEY'S BALL, Philippa awoke feeling refreshed and rather excited. Being back in the London scene had been more invigorating than anticipated. Last night she'd become reacquainted with some of the men who had courted her before her marriage, and she'd met many she had not been allowed an introduction to when she was a debutante. Most of the latter had been of higher rank than those she had been introduced to during her last Season; being the Dowager Countess of Essex made her a much more desirable acquaintance than a plain tradesman's daughter, no matter how large her dowry had been.

He had been the highest-ranking person she'd known before, and their meeting had been pure happenstance at one of the many balls she'd attended. Back then she'd thought he didn't care about the difference in their social stations. And perhaps he truly did not at first, but in the end he'd chosen his parents and his lofty bloodlines over her love, and had demonstrated exactly how low she ranked in his heart.

Banishing thoughts of *him*, hating that he loomed over

her entrée back into Society, Philippa got out of bed as her maid, Rose, came bustling in.

"Good morning, my lady," Rose said cheerfully. Rose was always chipper—it was one of the reasons Philippa had hired her. There was nothing like a cheerful countenance to lift one's own spirits. "The weather is beautiful today."

Making small talk, Philippa allowed Rose to dress her as she wished—sometimes she felt more like Rose's life-size doll than Rose's mistress—and arrange her hair in a simple but flattering style before she went down to breakfast. The household staff was already up and moving, what there was of them. Philippa had not felt the need for a full staff, as she and her companion Katherine Parrish were the only two in residence. At the age of eight and twenty, Katherine considered herself a spinster and happy to be so. She was rather pretty in a quiet way, but despite five Seasons in London she had not made a match.

Philippa thought this was partly due to Katherine's lack of dowry and partly due to her personality, which would only allow her to marry a man who acknowledged her as his intellectual equal. A small smile curved Philippa's lips at the thought, as she had yet to meet any man who actually *was* Katherine's equal. Her friend was more than a bit of a bluestocking, and her parents had encouraged their children to follow their own paths, which Katherine had certainly done. While she might be considered improperly outspoken and overly bookish, she had quite a good enough reputation to be Philippa's companion. And besides, Philippa no longer needed to slavishly devote herself to being a proper young miss.

Indeed, she planned on being quite improper. Discreet, of course, but definitely improper.

"Good morning dear, is your head feeling any better?" Philippa asked. Katherine had missed the ball last night, claiming a megrim, although Philippa had a strong suspicion that she'd spent the evening poring over the new book she'd purchased yesterday.

"Oh quite," Katherine said. "Did you enjoy yourself? Did you meet anyone interesting?" Her dark eyes sparkled with interest. Despite her spinster ways, Philippa suspected that Katherine had a romantic's soul. She was quite enthusiastic about Philippa's amorous goals, possibly living a bit vicariously, although she thought that Philippa should confine herself to one man and preferably marry him after falling head over heels in love.

Ha.

Philippa wasn't going to fall into either of those traps again, neither marriage nor love. Neither had made her happy, although at least her marriage had brought her some pleasure.

But that pleasure was perfectly possible without the marriage.

"Quite a few interesting men," Philippa responded with a smile. "Some of them may call on me today." She truly hoped that they did, although of course she'd have to be delicate about the nature of her desires. While she very much wanted a lover, she did not want to become an outcast of Society.

One of the gentlemen who had stood out to her last night was Conyngham. Strangely, for all his reputation as a rake, he was apparently quite discreet. His name was paired with so many ladies it was impossible to know which ones he had truly dabbled with.

People might gossip a bit if she was seen with him, but

no one would *know*. And despite his engaging smile and very good looks, Philippa knew that she could guard her heart with him.

There was quite a bit of freedom in being a wealthy widow of good social standing, although of course, as a tradesman's daughter, she was unlikely to ever receive the most elite invitations. But she was quite content with her position. After all, if she moved in the most elite circles there would be a much greater chance of running into *him*. Or his parents. Neither of which appealed.

"Well, you look lovely today," said Katherine.

"As do you," Philippa returned, grinning mischievously as she looked over Katherine's pretty burgundy morning dress with its creamy trim. It went very well with her dark hair and eyes, giving her a rosy flush to her cheeks. "You must take care not to steal any of my especial favorites away from me when they come calling."

"Oh pish," said Katherine with a merry laugh. "You know very well that I will not be any competition for you. I might dress well enough, but I was never and would never have been considered a Diamond of the First Water like yourself."

"Which means that you are all the more likely to find a man who will appreciate who you truly are and not just what you look like," Philippa said. She did not think that any of her inner sadness or bitterness had leaked into her voice, but Katherine gave her such a deep, searching look that she knew she had not been entirely successful in hiding it. Perhaps it was inevitable that her return to Society would be plagued with thoughts of *him*; the self-doubts that she was afflicted with had begun with him after all, even if they had finished with her husband.

But Philippa intended to use her appearance to her advantage now.

"Pay no mind to me," she said, waving her hand at Katherine as she turned to load her plate with tidbits from the sideboard. Philippa always had a healthy appetite in the morning, especially after a night of dancing. Piling on the sausage, kippers, and eggs, she situated herself at the table across from Katherine so they were facing each other as they chatted.

Later, she would wonder if all her thoughts of *him* had been a premonition.

At ten o'clock on the dot, all manner of flowers began to arrive, tokens from gentlemen that she'd spoken to or danced with the night before. Katherine and Philippa read through the attached notes with delight, giggling over her many conquests like giddy girls in their first Season.

Then a large arrangement of daffodils and rain flowers arrived, the white and yellow lilies making a spray of lighter color against the bright daffodils. Katherine looked at it and blinked.

"Daffodils for unrequited love or uncertainty, and are those *rain flowers?*" Her tone was incredulous, as it should be. In the language of flowers, which every young woman was well versed in, it made a blatant statement; begging for forgiveness, atoning for sins of the past, a blatant statement of love, and a plea that it be returned.

Philippa felt her pulse pounding as she picked up the card. Her name was written on it in a bold script that she thought she had forgotten. *Pippa,* it said on the envelope. Just seeing her shortened name made her chest clench in remembered anguish, and she could almost hear his voice in her ear. Katherine watched in somber silence as she broke the seal and read it.

The message was very simple: *You looked beautiful last night.*

There was no need to write anything else. The flowers said the rest. He had seen her last night. He knew that she had returned.

And, apparently, he wanted her forgiveness.

Suddenly furious, Philippa began to rip the paper into halves, and then halves again, and all the way down to tiny pieces until she dropped them to the floor. They drifted down gently, but the words could not be erased from her mind. She glared at the flowers.

It was a beautiful arrangement, but what it represented was loathsome. The urge to snatch up the vase and dash it against the wall rose up inside of her.

"Are you all right?" Katherine asked, placing delicate fingers on Philippa's upper arms.

When had her eyes begun to sting and water? Philippa drew in several deep breaths, calming herself, and forced a smile on her lips. It felt as false as his love had proved to be.

The cad.

How dare *he?* Philippa pushed the thought away. It did not matter what he did. What he said. He was nothing to her anymore. *Nothing.*

"Yes . . . I'm sorry." She eyed the flowers with distaste. "These can't stay here." She looked down at the scattered pieces of the note that had accompanied it and her mouth twisted.

"I'll ring for Morris," Katherine murmured.

When the butler arrived, Philippa directed the place-ment of flowers around the room where she would be receiving, stopping when she came to the daffodils and rain flowers. They really were quite beautiful . . . but she did not trust the message at all. And even if it were true, it was far too late.

"The trash bin," she said dismissively, before sweeping from the room.

The drawing room was filled with gentleman callers, more than Philippa would have thought possible for a widow such as herself. Of course, she knew that not every man there had honorable intentions, as evidenced by some of their sly innuendos, but that was the point. There were a few who seemed to be leaning toward romancing her rather than seducing her, and she made note of which was which.

She did not want to accidentally encourage those with romantic aspirations. Her own intentions were thoroughly dishonorable.

Still, even with dishonorable intentions, she had her standards. The Earl of Shaftesbury, for example, had no appeal for her. He was a fairly handsome man with dark blond hair and deep blue eyes, but he was married. There was no attraction on her side, and the way he watched her from across the room, with an almost hungry look, was unsettling.

By the end of the afternoon, she and Katherine were quite exhausted. Because of the large number of callers, Katherine had been just as busy conversing, entertaining those gentlemen who were unable to get close enough to Philippa's conversation. Actually, Philippa was quite sure that she'd lost at least two of her more romantic admirers to her friend—they'd seemed entranced by her wit and intellect, rather than repelled by it.

"Well dearest," Katherine said, after the last gentleman had been shown from the room. "That was quite an afternoon! When you said last night was successful, I had no idea."

"It was an unexpected crush," Philippa admitted. "I did not expect so many callers so quickly, I must confess."

The distraction had been very welcome, however. She had not thought about *him* once, other than a distinct feeling of relief when the afternoon had ended and he had not appeared. As the son of a duke, he could have certainly forced her hand by appearing on her doorstep while her drawing room was full of the *ton*. Publicly turning him away would have caused a scandal she could not possibly overcome.

Pressing her lips together, she realized she was filling her thoughts with him *again*.

"What did you think of Mr. Horn?" she asked Katherine.

He'd been among the most flirtatious of her suitors, and she found him very attractive. Witty without being cruel, engaging without being overly verbose, and handsome in his own right. Nephew to a duke, he was out of the line of heirs, and had proceeded to make his own way in the world, which she admired.

Despite knowing very little about him other than what she'd learned directly from him this afternoon, she'd accepted his invitation for a carriage ride later in the week. Carriages were supposed to be lovely venues for seduction, were they not? She sincerely hoped their goals aligned in that respect.

To her surprise, Katherine pursed her lips. Not in disapproval, but more like contemplation. "I ah, may have overheard something about him that I am afraid I do not quite understand," she confessed.

Which meant it was likely something salacious. Philippa had shared some of her knowledge about the marriage bed with her friend, but it was surprisingly hard to speak of in a frank manner. Explaining certain details was just too embarrassing. Especially when she also had to admit that *yes*, although it sounded awkward and messy, she'd quite enjoyed it.

Philippa tilted her head in inquiry, encouraging Katherine to continue. Brow furrowed in confusion and embarrassment, Katherine's expression held a pleading appeal— both wanting to understand what she had overheard and desiring Philippa not hold her curiosity against her.

"Two of the gentlemen near me saw Mr. Horn's interest in you and one of them shook his head and said they were all out of the running, for none of them could match his tongue. I do not think they were speaking of his wit, and I thought perhaps kissing, but it seemed as though he were indicating something *more*. I cannot imagine what else they were referring to."

A hot blush filled Philippa's cheeks. This was one of those acts that she had avoided speaking of with Katherine, who had been incensed by the idea that Philippa had used her own mouth on her husband. Since Katherine had a self-proclaimed abhorrence of even touching herself between her legs, Philippa could only imagine what this revelation would do to her sensibilities.

Clearing her throat, she tried to speak as dispassionately as possible, hoping to save herself some embarrassment by pretending to be unaffected. "Sometimes, as part of the, ah, marriage act, a man will use his tongue, um . . ." She gestured toward her skirts. Katherine blinked, confusion in her dark eyes. Philippa steeled herself. "He uses his tongue between her legs."

The words hung between them. Katherine blinked again, and then horror struck her expression when Philippa's meaning became clear. "No! Really? But . . . why?"

"Because it feels lovely," Philippa said wistfully. Clarence had not used his tongue in that manner enough as far as she was concerned. On their wedding night he had introduced her to its appeal, but it had certainly not been a frequent occurrence after that.

"It sounds . . . unhygienic." Katherine pursed her lips together and then shook her head. "I cannot imagine it. I am not even sure I wish to."

Laughing, Philippa gave her friend a sly look. "To think, in a few years you will be so firmly on the shelf that you may take a lover if you wish, and then he might want to use his tongue there!"

Katherine huffed. "Well, that is certainly one point against taking a lover."

Giggling madly, Philippa slouched back against the settee, not caring if she ruined her hair. It would need to be redone before the evening anyway. She was so glad Katherine had come with her to London; life would be much more dreary without her.

CHAPTER FOUR

"ARE YOU TRYING TO LOSE?" CONYNGHAM asked, clearly puzzled, scooping his winnings in front of him.

Disgusted with himself, Everett threw down his cards, shaking his head. While he could certainly afford the money, he did not enjoy losing. All of his friends seemed baffled at his poor playing. But he could not concentrate.

Had not been able to concentrate since he'd sent the flowers to Pippa.

Had not been able to stop wondering how she had reacted when she received his long overdue apology and declaration of love. Relief? Tears of joy? Sadness?

There had been no return note for him, although he'd waited all afternoon. Perhaps she was still angry with him. It had been years, though. She'd been married and widowed. Surely if he could forgive her time in another man's bed, she could forgive him for his part in placing her there. Especially once he explained that his kiss with Lady Alice had been an attempt to make her jealous, to make her regret *her* words.

With the wisdom of several years behind him, Everett

now understood that Pippa must have been frightened when she made her ultimatum. In his bleakest moment, he'd thought she'd been frightened of losing access to his title . . . but she'd married into the nobility and then done nothing with her new position. She'd eschewed Society entirely. Despite his mother's claims, he did not think Pippa had been a title hunter.

"Everett?" Roger sounded cautious, and Everett realized he'd been sitting in silence, staring blankly at nothing.

Standing abruptly, he pushed back his chair. "I need a drink."

The others looked at each other and Conyngham shrugged. "I think we could all use a moment."

Several of his friends drifted out onto the patio, likely to take in some fresh air, while Everett made his way to the drink service. Pouring himself a liberal snifter of brandy, he tried to shake loose thoughts of Pippa. Tomorrow he'd send her some perfume, or perhaps some jewelry, and continue to shower presents on her from afar until she was eagerly anticipating being in his presence so she could properly thank him.

Twit. The insult whispered through his head, puncturing some of his confidence. *Do you really think she wants anything to do with you at all?*

But Everett had not been raised to suffer bouts of self-doubt. He had been raised to succeed. If he wanted something, he worked until he got it. And with something he wanted so badly—marriage to Pippa—he refused to give in to any thoughts that might lead to failure.

Either way, jewelry could certainly not go amiss. He had scorned her after all, though he had not meant to. He had been young and stupid, but there was no doubt that he'd hurt her. He hoped it was true that time healed all wounds.

A heavy hand coming down on his shoulder jolted him back out of his thoughts. Turning to face Roger's grim visage, Everett sighed. He'd been avoiding his friend ever since the ball where the wager for Pippa's affections had been set. So far Roger had not revealed Everett's past with Pippa to the others, thankfully, but he was sure Roger wished to.

"If I hazard a guess as to the reason for your distraction, will you lose more money this evening?" Roger asked dryly.

Pushing a rueful smile onto his face, Everett shrugged, pretending a nonchalance he did not feel. "I would never accept such a wager from you."

They'd been friends for too long, and Roger knew him too well. He was often able to guess what was on Everett's mind. The expression on Roger's face grew more serious.

"You should never have accepted the wager over Pippa," Roger said quietly, ensuring none of their friends would overhear. His blue eyes were full of worry, clearly anxious over what Pippa's return might mean for Everett's state of mind.

Everett had hoped that avoiding this discussion and allowing Roger to *see* how unaffected he was would negate the need to assuage Roger's concerns. Mostly because he did not want to hear Roger's concerns. He did not want to hear anyone's. Last time Pippa had been in his grasp, he'd lost her because of his parents.

This time he was going to be strong enough to stand beside her, no matter who tried to pry them apart.

"I'll win it, *and* her," he said firmly, taking a sip of his drink. The burn of the alcohol down his throat was satisfying, fortifying him for what lay ahead.

"Until she discovers you wagered on it," Roger muttered.

Frowning, Everett focused on his friend. "What has that to do with anything?"

Looking at him blankly, Roger stared for a moment and then shook his head. "Sometimes I forget you know nothing about wooing a woman."

"Of course I know how to woo a woman," Everett said, insulted. At this point in his life, his reputation was such that no one should doubt his prowess. Especially not when the stakes actually mattered, like now.

Roger snorted and Everett bristled. Holding up his hand, Roger shook his head. "No, hear me out. I am not denying that you are adept at wooing a lover or a mistress . . . but a woman you wish to marry? You have never even made the attempt, and it is a very different kind of courting."

How different could it possibly be? Everett's frown deepened. "Are you having me on?" he asked suspiciously.

With a groan, Roger tossed back his entire brandy and turned away, shaking his head and muttering to himself. "Dear lord, give me strength. This is going to be a right bloody mess."

Rather than calling him back, Everett let him stalk away. He clearly needed time to compose himself. He'd see in the end.

Different.

Everett snorted. Pippa had fallen in love with him once before, so the foundation was already there. Now that she was a widow, he did not need to be as circumspect as he had been before, either. He would use every trick in his arsenal to engage her, get her into his bed, and once he'd seduced her then he could propose. The little niggle of doubt tried to creep back into his mind, but he swept it away. He would not allow doubt to sway him again.

His parents would wail and bluster, but he was a grown man. While they might threaten his inheritance, he had his own interests these days. His income did not rely solely on the estate, unlike his father's. Quietly investing money in trade, no matter how lowbrow his mother found it, had made him a fortune. If they left him with nothing but the entailed estates, which were his by birthright, he and Pippa would still prosper.

Once he knew her reaction to the flowers, he could make his plans from there, claim his love, and win the wager.

One thing Everett had not counted on was his difficulty in *finding* Pippa again.

He had no desire to join the scramble of gentlemen flocking to her drawing room during the afternoons she was at home. There he would be one of many, and there would be no opportunity to sneak her away for a private moment. Sharing her attention was not part of his plan. He needed a venue where they could speak more intimately, he could explain the past, and they could begin their courtship anew.

With the Season in full swing, there were various balls and routs every evening, and guests rarely stayed at one the entire night. Guessing which one Pippa would be at had turned out to be nigh impossible for several nights in a row. His only comfort was that Conyngham was similarly frustrated, going by the reports of their friends.

Every night, Roger was at Everett's side, grimly sallying forth despite the marriage-minded mothers of the *ton* who accosted him on behalf of their daughters, and sighing with relief every time Pippa was not in attendance. There was nothing to do but grin and bear it, until finally, *finally,* her name was announced at Shaftesbury House. The earl and his countess had twittered over the coup of Everett appearing at their "little soiree," and he'd been obliged to remain for a few hours.

He'd chosen this gathering out of sheer luck, not actually expecting to see Pippa there, as there were far more important balls to attend this evening—the Duchess of Cornwall's *and* Lady Cowper's—but he'd decided to try a smaller event first. Beside him, Roger groaned as Everett's head snapped around, like a hound scenting its prey.

There she was, at the top of the stairs with Olivia, the Marchioness of Hertford, at her side. They made as good an entrance as they had when they'd first debuted—light and dark beside each other, Lady Dawn and Lady Twilight they'd been called. Pippa's dark hair was coiled around her head and glittering with jewels. The deep blue of her gown glittered with more jewels, making her appear an embodiment of the night sky. Beside her, Olivia was the sunrise, blonde curls adorned with roses and feathers, her rose and cream gown making her even brighter next to Pippa's dramatic dark.

Together they were stunning, but Everett only had eyes for one of them.

His feet were moving without thinking and, as Pippa descended the stairs, she glanced up. Their eyes caught. Held. The expression on her face blanked, like a mask, covering her reaction to seeing him. Something tightened inside of Everett's chest, bringing him to an abrupt halt.

Turning her head away without acknowledging him, Pippa's lips curved in a smile at something Olivia said to her.

She cut me.

No one knew. It had not been obvious.

But she had *seen* him and . . . and had not acknowledged him.

"Oh, here we go," Roger muttered, but Everett barely registered the words. He was still reeling with the shock of Pippa's lack of response to his presence.

Turning to face his friend, he kept his voice low so as not to be overheard, but he needed to know he wasn't imagining things. "She saw me, did she not? She looked right at me . . . she *saw* me."

"She did," Roger confirmed. Then he sighed at the expression on Everett's face. "I told you this would not be as easy as you thought. Clearly she's still angry."

So it would seem.

"You were right," he said, rubbing his chin with some consternation. Perhaps Roger's advice had been sounder than he'd initially thought. Clearly, Pippa was going to need more to earn her forgiveness. There was a very small part of him that balked at the idea, but he'd sworn that Pippa would be his again.

Pride had been part of his downfall before; he had no use for it now.

Damn and blast.

She knew she shouldn't have come to the Shaftesbury ball.

But she had not been invited to the more august

surrounds of Lady Cowper's or the Duchess of Cornwall's, of course, and Mr. Horn had said he would be in attendance at Shaftesbury House. Philippa had thought the opportunity to see him again before their carriage ride tomorrow was fortuitous, even though she did not care for Lord Shaftesbury. While she knew many gentlemen and ladies of the *ton* took lovers outside of their marriages, it was impossible to tell whether or not it caused their spouse pain.

Philippa had told herself she did not mind Clarence's mistresses, but his need for them still preyed on her mind, nibbling at her confidence. If she'd held him in any greater regard than affection, she could not imagine how painful knowledge of his other lovers would have been. Ironically, or perhaps hypocritically, he had preferred her not to have other lovers. She had not minded at the time, but now she was determined to experience all the *ton* had to offer.

As long as what it had to offer was not married.

And was not *him*.

There was a part of her that exulted in his presence. Not because she particularly wanted to see him, but because of the look on his face when he'd seen her in all her glory. She might not be his social equal still, but their positions were no longer so disparate.

She also knew she looked particularly stunning tonight.

Which he clearly appreciated, from the awe in his expression. Shock, awe, longing, desire—everything she would have said she wanted to see. Well, perhaps she could do with a bit more regret over losing her. That may come later.

Smugness warred with trepidation, and she was grateful when Olivia whispered in her ear, pulling her attention away from *him*.

"I almost feel as though I am debuting again," Olivia giggled.

"Just don't allow the men to court you or Francis will have a fit," Philippa teased back, turning away from *him*. He did not matter anyway. Tonight she was going to dance and flirt with as many gentlemen as she pleased, tomorrow she was going on a carriage ride with Mr. Horn, and the day after the Duke of Beaufort would be joining her for lunch.

Olivia's husband had decided to stay in tonight. Unlike his wife, he found constant socializing to be a bore; although he made an effort to join her regularly, he did not have the constitution to bear up every night and had gratefully handed her off into Philippa's and Katherine's care. Although Katherine had insisted on walking behind them down the stairs so as not to ruin their grand entrance.

At some point during the Season, Philippa was going to ensure her lovely companion was pushed out of the shadows she hid in.

"I'm sure the gentlemen will be much more interested in you," Olivia teased back as they reached the bottom of the stairs.

Her words were practically prophetic, as an absolute crush of gentlemen surged forward to make themselves known to Philippa. Laughing delightedly, she allowed herself to be pulled into their circle. Keeping Olivia and Katherine by her side, she moved her admirers to the side of the ballroom where they could converse more easily.

The eager banter of the gentlemen distracted her so well that she forgot *he* was also in attendance until she stepped out onto the dance floor with Lord Brooke and saw *him* watching her from across the way. Skimming her gaze over the guests, pretending she had not seen *him* at all, again, she turned to face Lord Brooke. The lord was a rather serious man, handsome, and she was fairly certain he was looking for a wife and not a lover, but he was also an excellent dancer.

If he began to look at her more seriously for a wife, she might have to dissuade him. Fortunately, the cotillon made conversation nearly impossible, and she could lose herself in the steps, gliding gracefully across the floor.

Once the dance was over, Lord Brooke began to escort her back to her circle when the second gentleman she'd least like to speak to stepped in front of them. Unfortunately, as he was their host, she had no choice but to greet him.

"Dare I hope you have room left on your dance card?" Lord Shaftesbury asked flirtatiously. Philippa pressed her lips together, summoning her social graces so she did not inadvertently show her disdain.

"Unfortunately not, my lord," she said prettily. "Your other guests have been most welcoming."

"How could they not, with such a beauty in our midst?" There was something of a leer in Shaftesbury's eyes, which made Lord Brooke shift uncomfortably and made Pippa wish her décolletage was a touch less revealing.

"We should return to them, so I am not thought rude," Philippa said with a little laugh, squeezing Lord Brooke's arm slightly, hoping he took her hint. "If you will excuse us, my lord."

While Lord Brooke seemed to understand, Shaftesbury did not.

"I will escort you back," he said, stepping to her other

side, and looking at Lord Brooke over her head. "My wife was hoping to speak with you, Gabriel. She's just over there, by the drinks."

With that, Shaftesbury neatly cut off any avenue of escape. To deny his escort would be supremely insulting. Sometimes the social mores of the *ton* really were such a bother. Philippa bit her tongue against chiding his presumptuousness. Walking round the room on his arm would not be such a chore, and once she was back with Olivia, Katherine, and her gentlemen admirers, it would be easy to focus her attention on the others without being rude.

Lord Brooke bowed over Philippa's hand and left her in Lord Shaftesbury's care. *One arm is the same as another*, she told herself, but it wasn't true. Especially when he put his fingers over hers in far too familiar a manner. Thankfully they were both wearing gloves; she would not have liked to feel his skin against hers, even just on her hand.

"You must be very pleased with the turnout this evening," she remarked, an opening gambit designed to keep their conversation to the innocuous.

But Shaftesbury was no novice to the game, unlike herself.

"Since it brought you to my doorstep, I must be," he said, his body coming closer to hers.

Philippa stiffened her arm, doing her best to keep the space between them. Unlike when she was a debutante, there would be no chaperone running in to rescue her. If she could catch Katherine's eye, her companion would certainly oblige; but unlike a chaperone, Katherine wasn't always watching, and she was currently half a room away. Seeing each other was difficult enough, much less making eye contact.

Shaftesbury also seemed determined to take a route closer to the wall, away from the dance floor, which Philippa did not resist at first until she realized how many secluded little resting nooks were located there. They were meant for resting tired feet, but they also provided an opportunity for private conversation that the rest of the ballroom did not.

If she had an interest at all in Shaftesbury, she might have been impressed by his maneuver; but she was not interested, and she had not done anything to indicate she would be. Frustration welled up inside of her. The man had a perfectly beautiful young wife; why wasn't he paying these attentions to her? A question she'd asked herself of Clarence multiple times . . . a question that had arisen even before she'd married Clarence because of *him*.

"Lord Shaftesbury, my circle is over there." She gestured with her fan, trying to inject some steel into her voice. Either she failed or he was immune to the censure.

"I will return them to you directly," he said, with what she imagined he thought was a charming smile. "I thought you might want to sit down and rest your feet for a moment."

"I appreciate your concern, but my feet are eager to return to the dance floor," she riposted, vainly trying to move him in the direction she wished to go. But he was larger, stronger, and more practiced at such maneuvers; he resisted her attempt at redirection quite easily. Philippa's voice began to rise in frustration. "I do not want my next partner to think me rude."

"I will offer him an explanation," Lord Shaftesbury reassured her, and Philippa clenched her teeth against a scream of frustration.

Why would he not take the hint?

"Ah, there you are Pippa." The deep, smooth voice was just as she remembered, and Philippa's breath caught in her throat. "It is almost time for our dance."

She whirled around and there *he* was, mere feet away, darkly handsome and impeccably turned out. At this close distance, it was impossible to pretend she had not seen him or to turn away.

Everett Cavendish, Marquess of Hartington, heir to the Duke of Devonshire, and the only man to ever hold and break her heart, held out his hand.

CHAPTER FIVE

TO EVERETT, IT WAS CLEAR THAT PIPPA HAD no wish for Shaftesbury's escort—and why. What was unclear was whether or not she would accept his rescue. While the expression on her face had turned blank and unreadable when she'd seen him earlier, now her confliction was obvious. She might not want to follow Shaftesbury's lead, but she did not wish for Everett's either.

When she let go of Shaftesbury's arm and reached for his hand, he felt pure triumph swell inside of him. Only slightly because she had chosen him, but mostly because now she was trapped with him for the length of a dance. Now they could finally speak.

Her gloved fingers settled against his, and he swore he could feel a chill even through the fabric. Another chill was emanating from Shaftesbury, who did not dare contradict the highest-ranking guest in his house, but who clearly wanted to. Well he could find some other beauty to focus his seduction on.

This beauty was Everett's to seduce.

Even if it appeared his journey was going to be more arduous than he'd initially realized.

"I did not realize you were acquainted," Shaftesbury said. His question was directed at Pippa, but it was Everett who answered.

"From years ago," Everett replied smoothly. "But I could never forget Lady Twilight." Her lips tightened but she did not gainsay his claim. The violins sounded, indicating the next song was about to start.

"Thank you for your escort, Lord Shaftesbury," she said with a slight curtsey, obviously wanting to end the conversation.

"My lady." He bowed, but his eyes glinted with displeasure.

Everett gave him a nod and began herding Pippa toward the dance floor. If Shaftesbury had been a bit stiff, she was as rigid as a fence post on his arm. The air felt almost chilly around them, as if she were changing the temperature by sheer force of will.

He realized he had absolutely no idea what to say to her.

A few notes of music drifted through the air, calling the dancers to the center of the ballroom, and Everett smiled.

A waltz.

Somewhere, Lady Luck was smiling down on him.

Of course it was a waltz.

She *should* be dancing with Mr. Theodore Branch, but there was no hope of rescue from that quarter. Even if Mr. Branch came looking for her, he would immediately understand that he'd been supplanted by the son of a duke, and she doubted he would even complain. Very few men would dare to.

There was nothing to be done but follow the marquess's escort onto the floor and get into position, her gaze firmly fixed above his shoulder, and wait for the music to begin. The feel of her hand in his, the way his fingers settled around her waist, felt all too familiar and far too intimate.

Philippa imagined ice sheering down her insides, cooling her, calming her, and making her impervious to his touch.

"Did you receive my flowers?" he asked softly, his voice low and meant for her ears only.

"I did." Her reply was short. Clipped.

"And did you understand the message?"

"I did."

The music started, swelling, and *he* stepped forward, guiding her backward and then whirling aggressively enough to take her breath away. Still, she kept up with him easily, her long legs stretching to match his steps, her skirts intertwining with his legs. There was a reason the waltz had been considered too scandalous when it first came upon the social scene.

"Then why did you not respond?" There was aggrieved frustration in his voice as well as confusion, and it took every ounce of willpower that Philippa possessed not to deliberately trod on his foot. If she thought it would do any good, she wouldn't have been able to resist.

"Some men might take the lack of a response *as* the response," she said tartly, still not looking at him. He was watching her though. She could see him out of the corner of her eye.

A skilled dancer, he guided her through the steps, keeping them away from the other dancers, even without his full attention on their path across the floor. If he were any other man, she would be enjoying herself immensely. Because he was *him,* every step felt like she was dangling over a precipice, waiting for the inevitable fall.

"I *am* sorry," he said, leaning forward to purr the words in her ear. His hot breath slid over her skin, and Philippa's spine stiffened against her body's immediate reaction.

Whatever her feelings for him, the attraction between them had not diminished at all. Not from time, nor space, nor his betrayal. It was infuriating to be betrayed by her own body, but Philippa pushed it all away. Surely, once she had a lover, or lovers, the attraction would diminish. She'd been attracted to other gentlemen this week as well. It meant nothing.

The tender look in his eyes meant nothing too. So did his apology.

"Consider yourself forgiven," she said, her voice as stiff as her spine.

"Then can we begin our acquaintance anew?" Flirtation colored his tone, and Philippa almost recoiled in horror.

"*No!*" She said the word loudly enough that the couple beside them looked over at her. Pushing a strained smiled onto her lips, she nodded at them and looked away, lowering her voice so only Hartington—she refused to think of him by his Christian name, his title was bad enough—could hear her. "Forgiven, but not forgotten. I have no wish for *any* kind of acquaintance with you."

The pure venom in Pippa's vehement declaration took him aback for a moment.

His own frustration pricked at him, but he ignored it. Those impulses were how he had lost her in the first place.

64

He was no longer a callow youth full of reckless pride; he was a man, and he wanted to win back the woman he'd lost. Which meant acknowledging that perhaps he had hurt her even more deeply than he'd realized at the time.

"What if I wish to make it up to you?" he asked quietly.

"The best way to make anything up to me is to leave me alone."

Despite her ire, Everett felt compelled to point out that she'd chosen him over Shaftesbury. "If I had left you alone, you would be having an intimate conversation with our host right now instead of me."

Because he was holding her so closely, he could feel the shudder that went through her body, even though her expression did not change. "Very well. If you see me in need of rescue from an importuning gentleman, you may intervene, as any true gentleman would. Have a care that *you* do not becoming the importuning gentleman."

Despite her sharp words, there was a kind of fragility about her, and Everett realized that both could likely be laid at his feet. While Pippa could be tart when the occasion called for it, her nature had been sweet. Open. Trusting. Now her expression was closed, there was a cynicism to her nature that had not been present before her marriage, and the trust was completely gone.

Could he really blame her?

For the first time, he truly questioned whether or not he'd be able to win a place back in her heart. The small doubts that had tried to creep into his mind before raised up like a hydra . . . but the stakes were too high for him to retreat so easily. Not the stakes for his bet with Conyngham, but the stakes for his life. He wanted Pippa as his wife and no other.

"I cannot do that, Pippa," he murmured. If he'd thought she was stiff before, that was nothing compared to the way she turned into an ice block in his arms at the use of her nickname. "I lost you once. I don't mean to again."

"You cannot lose what you toss away." The cutting edge of her voice was brittle, but for the first time she was meeting his gaze, her blue eyes filled with fury and hurt.

"I was a blunderbuss. I did not mean to toss you away, only to show you that . . . that you could not control me with ultimatums. That I had other options as well. I was angry when you said you would accept another's proposal if I took too long."

"Well you showed me very well, and now I don't mean to accept any proposals that aren't thoroughly indecent." Something in her eyes flared.

It took Everett a moment to realize her meaning, and his own emotions flared at her blatant announcement. He immediately understood she meant to prod him, to anger him. The years had eased his temper though. She would not so easily chase him off.

"I am happy to offer you an indecent proposal until you are ready for a respectable one," he countered.

Pippa stumbled and he caught her, keeping them moving smoothly through the steps. The incredulous look she gave him suddenly turned to suspicion. "I am not interested in tying myself to any *one* man, even for pleasure."

Possessiveness surged, jealousy churned his insides, but Everett forced himself to keep calm. She wanted a reaction. Anticipated driving him away with her words.

"Ah, so you will not mind if I have other lovers as well?"

"I do not care at all what you do," she said, so succinctly that he almost believed it. The ice falling off her in sheets told a different story, however. Despite her words, she was not unaffected. "But if you think to convince me to marry you, whilst you visit other pastures, you are sorely mistaken. If I *ever* marry again, it will be to a man who loves me, *truly* and *faithfully*."

Her hypocrisy stirred his anger in a way the rest of it had not.

"So I am to remain celibate while you take as many lovers as you please, or else you would not even consider my offer? Why should I not expect a true and faithful wife?"

Pippa laughed, but there was no humor in the sound. "Of the two of us, only one of us needs to prove their capability of faithfulness. I was true and faithful to you, until you cast me aside for Lady Alice. And I was true and faithful to my husband, despite *his* mistresses and lovers. *I* do not wish to convince you to marry me. Therefore, I am under no obligation to continue to prove myself to you. But if you truly wish to marry me, then visiting another woman's bed will do nothing but show me how little you've changed."

The music ended, his mind whirling with the implications of her words.

Nothing she had said was wrong, but it *felt* wrong. How could he possibly allow her to take other lovers while he focused his efforts on courting her with an eye to marriage? But how could he convince her otherwise when she was right on all counts?

"I'll win you back," he said, the words almost a threat. "I still love you, Pippa. I always have."

She gave him a long look, the fire gone from her eyes. They had turned sad instead, with such a lonely sadness that it made his heart ache. That was when he finally realized, she truly did not expect him to keep his word. She did not believe him.

He had betrayed her before and then her husband had as well. Pippa had given her heart to one man, her body to another, and neither had been faithful to her. No wonder she did not mean to marry again, or even to have a single lover.

It did not matter what he said or what promises he made; he'd made and broken promises to her before. It did not matter how he professed his love to her; he'd told her so before and then kissed another woman where she was sure to see. Now he understood. His words meant nothing. It was his behavior that had broken her heart and it was only by his actions that he would gain her trust and love again.

Even if it meant watching her succumb to the seduction of other men, while he turned away the affections of other women. It was a Herculean task, one that would test his temper, his pride, and his self-control. But it would also prove to her, without a doubt, that he loved her, no matter what.

Pippa turned away, and he did not know whether she heard his final words to her or not.

"I will prove myself to you, Pippa. I swear it."

As soon as she returned to her circle, Olivia and Katherine rushed up to her, crowding her from either side and providing a much-needed buffer from the other gentlemen. Facing off against Hartington had left her feeling bruised. The walls she'd tried to throw up were battered and thin, especially in the face of his confessions.

Not that she believed him.

She could not.

The very idea that he was still in love with her was ludicrous. If he had *ever* loved her. But hearing the words from him again . . . she felt as though she'd been dragged through the streets of London by a runaway horse. Every inch of her was chafed raw from the encounter.

"Oh my goodness, I am so sorry," Olivia said, her fingers pressing against Philippa's for a quick moment. "I almost fainted when I saw you on the dance floor with *him*. I could not think how to intervene without Francis here to assist. None of the other gentlemen . . ."

None of the other gentlemen would dare to cut in on the Marquess of Hartington.

"I know," Philippa said gently, giving her friend a smile she did not entirely feel. But it was not Olivia's fault. There really had not been anything she could have done.

"Are you all right?" Katherine whispered.

"Fine. I am fine." If she admitted she was anything else, she was liable to fall apart. At least she could finally breathe again, away from Hartington's presence, even if her corset still felt a bit tight.

Still, she had come through it. Faced him, said her piece, and lived to tell the tale. Some of her raw edges were soothed by the realization. If—when—she encountered him again, surely it would be easier with the first face to face already out of the way. And because he had warned her, she could bolster her defenses against whatever lies and promises he made this time.

Eventually he would surely retreat. Especially when she found a lover. Or *lovers*. His pride would never allow him to pursue a wife who had another lover. Philippa nearly snorted at the idea. Apparently reminding him that there had been other men vying for her hand, men her father might accept, had sent him into another woman's arms.

If her father had accepted a suitor on her behalf, she would have needed a very good reason for not also accepting a proposal. That another gentleman claimed to love her but had not, and did not soon plan to, approach her father for her hand would not have been an acceptable reason. But Everett had seen her words as an ultimatum, a way of forcing his hand . . . and he'd responded by kissing Lady Alice Dormer.

If he continued to pursue Philippa after she'd taken a lover, she would eat her favorite hat.

Giving herself a little shake, a more genuine smile formed on her lips. The fastest way to be rid of *him* would be to find that lover. Or lovers. Perhaps as many lovers as she could manage. A little part of her saddened—the soft, sappy part of her heart that wished to give him another chance—but she ignored it. It would be for the best.

Looking past Olivia, she coquettishly tilted her head at Mr. Branch, who was still standing among her suitors. "I am so sorry, Mr. Branch, for missing our dance. The marquess was insistent."

"I understand, my lady," Mr. Branch said, with a slight bow. He really did look as though he understood, too. "Perhaps we could stroll the room now, instead?"

Still smiling, Philippa nodded her acquiescence and stepped forward. She did not miss the worried expressions on Olivia and Katherine's faces as she walked away, but they would soon realize she had everything under control.

CHAPTER SIX

"OPEN FOR ME, DARLING." CLARENCE'S VOICE was coaxing, seductive.

Shyly, Philippa spread her thighs. She blushed as Clarence stared down at her exposed private area, his gaze arrested by the sight of her wet curls and swollen folds.

"Beautiful," he murmured. Sliding his hands up her legs, his thumbs caressing her inner thighs, he pushed them even further apart, making her squeak at the immodesty of the position. Still, it excited her even further, to be so exposed to him. After all, he was her husband. There was nothing wrong with it, despite how indecent it felt.

Leaning down, he pressed his mouth to that hot, wet flesh, and Philippa gasped at the utterly wicked sensation. She moaned, closing her eyes and leaning her head back as Clarence laved his tongue over her sensitive flesh. Pleasure curled through her, traveling in rivulets along her senses.

"Oh Clarence . . ." She gasped, squirming, and reached down to thread her fingers through his hair.

But instead of the long strands she expected, her fingers met a shorter cut. Philippa's eyes flew open and she pulled on the suddenly black hair she was holding.

Everett rose over her, looking like a lord of sin, his eyes blazing as he gazed down at her.

"Pippa," he murmured, and he leaned down, swallowing her confused protest with a kiss.

Heat and need surged, and her hips tilted up to meet his cock as his tongue danced with hers. Philippa clung to him as he slid inside her, thick and filling, satisfying the cravings of her body. They rocked together, the small incredulous part of her drowned out by the growing sensations, the memory of Everett's voice ringing in her ears.

"Pippa . . . Pippa . . ."

He moved inside her, harder and faster, filling her over and over again. Philippa writhed beneath him, crying out . . . and waking herself up.

The need to climax was too strong, and she reached down to press her fingers against herself. As she rocked against them, ecstasy burst over her. Even now, in the darkness, it was Everett's face she saw as she gasped with pleasure, leaving her feeling ashamed and confused. Panting from the exertion, she rolled onto her side and clutched her pillow, still aware of the throbbing between her legs. Eventually, she finally managed to fall back asleep.

The next morning, she woke feeling more determined than ever to make the most out of her Season and to stay away from *him*. While she might not have been able to keep him out of her dreams last night, she would do her best to replace him in her mind with more palatable gentlemen. After breakfast, she and Katherine descended upon her wardrobe to decide on the best dress to wear for her carriage ride with Mr. Horn. Philippa did not know if he planned to seduce her or not, but she was hoping to make her own intentions plain to him.

Especially after what Katherine had overheard about his . . . predilections.

"It is remarkably freeing, being able to go on a carriage ride without a chaperone," Philippa confessed, pulling on her favorite pair of gloves. Their pale grey color went well with the red and grey dress she and Katherine had chosen for the ride. Mr. Horn was due to arrive at any moment. A cherry red hat with a grey feather finished off the ensemble.

"You are making me feel as though I should accompany you," Katherine said with a laugh, pinning the hat to Philippa's curls. "Am I being a poor companion by allowing you to run amuck so freely?"

"On the contrary," Philippa said, a wicked gleam in her bright eyes as she stood. "I believe it makes you the *perfect* companion."

"You will tell me all about it when you return?"

Philippa paused, then tilted her head at her friend and winked. "I supposed it depends on exactly what we do."

"Oh you." Katherine laughed again and stepped back, looking over Philippa with admiration. "Hm. Perhaps you have a point. I think any gentleman would be hard pressed to resist you looking like *that*."

Philippa could only hope so.

At exactly two o'clock, Mr. Horn knocked on the front door. Philippa did not keep him waiting. She whisked down the stairs as soon as the butler came for her, Katherine following behind her to watch his reaction. It was certainly gratifying, the way his hazel eyes widened, his gaze traveling over her trim figure and the cleavage she'd dared leave exposed.

The neckline was not scandalous, but it was certainly lower than most ladies would wear for a mere carriage ride. Not as low as a ballgown, however. Philippa and Katherine had decided it tread the perfect line between respectability and invitation.

"My lady," Mr. Horn said, stepping forward to take her hand and bowing over it. If his touch did not sear her in quite the same manner as Hartington's, that did not mean a thing. "You look stunning, as ever."

"And you are as handsome as ever," she returned. It was only the truth. He was impeccably turned out in a navy jacket, with a checkered vest, a crisp white shirt, and a beautifully tied cravat. Philippa's attraction to him was part of why she had agreed to a carriage ride, after all.

Mr. Horn escorted her out of the house and into his carriage. Philippa's heart beat a little faster when she saw that it was a closed carriage. Part of her had wondered if he might turn up in a curricle or phaeton. Both of which could be quite exciting and were an excellent opportunity to show off one's driving skills, but neither of which were an aid to seduction.

It seemed that perhaps Mr. Horn was already thinking along the same lines as herself.

He helped her into the carriage, letting her settle her skirts, before following and rapping the ceiling. At the sound, the carriage lurched forward, his driver directing the horses onto the street. The curtains were drawn back, allowing them to see the passing houses of Mayfair and the various people out for a promenade. The weather was fine with a nice breeze, so the carriage wouldn't be too stifling even if the curtains were drawn.

Did Philippa want the curtains to be drawn?

Was she going to allow Mr. Horn to seduce her if he was so inclined?

Before last night she would have said "Yes, absolutely." Now, Hartington had wormed his way into her thoughts even more so than before, making her question her direction. Then again, perhaps that was the strongest argument for moving ahead in her quest to find a lover. That he was already affecting her decisions did not bode well for the state of her mind—or heart.

To her disappointment, Mr. Horn's conversation was completely normal as the carriage moved through the streets. The close confines provided the illusion of intimacy and privacy, but he did not seem inclined to do anything with it. So when he asked if she had any hopes for the Season, she took the opening. Because she *had* come to London for a reason, and she was not going to let *him* and his likely false protestation of love divert her from her course.

"I must confess, I do hope to find a gentleman or two with whom I can form a . . . fond friendship," she said, her tone delicate but suggestive. Depending on how he responded, she might back away entirely, but she hoped she had not read him completely incorrectly. "I enjoyed country life, but without my husband it became rather . . . lonely."

To her delight, Mr. Horn's eyes gleamed at her words, his smile sharpening with intent. Leaning forward, he took her gloved hand in his, and Philippa's breath caught in her throat. *Oh my* . . . She'd gone from being impatient with his social niceties to feeling a bit like prey.

"I would very much like to be your . . . friend, my lady," he said.

"Please, call me Philippa, then," she said, curving her fingers slightly around his as well. As a debutante, such blatant physical contact would have been absolutely forbidden. She'd had a few stolen moments with *him* of course, but she'd always known they could not possibly lead to anything too intimate. Kisses, here and there, but at that time she had not been able to even imagine the multitude of possible affections between a man and a woman.

Now, knowing what could be, she found this interchange more exciting than she would have imagined. Triumph tinged her emotions as well—this had not been difficult at *all*.

"And you must call me Marcus," he responded immediately. "Did you not have any . . . especial friends out in the country?"

Philippa shook her head, and her heart leapt in her chest when he covered her hand with both of his and she felt his fingers begin to undo the buttons of her glove. Philippa had always waited for Clarence in her bed, already in her nightgown and ready for his visit, so she had never had the experience of a man undressing her, even in such a small way. It was thrilling, even if it was just a glove— made even more so by the way his eyes remained trained on hers, holding her gaze in an almost hypnotic stare.

"I . . . am not experienced with making friends," she confessed. Her lips parted in a little gasp when he pulled the glove from her hand and bent down over it. Instead of pressing his lips to the back of her hand though, he kissed the center of her palm, and arousal shot through her immediately.

No man had touched her so intimately since Clarence, and her body ached for it. Just the press of his lips was enough to rouse the need that had brought her to London to almost painful heights.

Lifting his head, Marcus met her eyes again. "And you are looking for *friends*, not a particular friend?"

Her body aflutter with needy sensations, it took Philippa a moment to realize what he was asking. "Yes! Oh, I mean, yes. I . . ."

With him holding her bare hand, gazing directly at her as if he could see into her soul, she could not find the words to discreetly explain her disinterest in being bound to one man. But it did not seem to matter.

"Perhaps we could close the curtains, and I could demonstrate my friendship," he murmured, with utterly wicked intent. Philippa's mouth went dry and she nodded, a short, sharp nod.

Her bravado had fled, leaving behind anticipation, excitement, and a tiny bit of fear. Not fear of Marcus, but fear of herself. Fear of disappointing him. Fear of discovering what it was about her that made both her first love and her first husband unable to be faithful. Unlike the other two, he had no reason to lie to her if she was less than satisfactory.

But she wanted this.

And she needed to know.

Even if the knowledge hurt, perhaps she could learn to be better.

The curtains fell, enclosing them in dim light that made the world feel a little less real . . . and then Marcus's lips were on hers.

Philippa gasped at her first kiss since Clarence. Her lips parted automatically, and Marcus's tongue delved in. His body pressed against hers, pushing her against the cushions of the seat. It was heady and exciting, and more than a little arousing.

She might not know what she was doing, but he certainly did.

Hands roamed over her dress, finding the buttons at the front and flicking them open to reveal her breasts. With her nipples budded into hard little nubs, Philippa moaned when flesh touched flesh. It felt as though her entire body was on fire, lit from within and burning hotter with every second.

The kiss went on and on as he devoured her, his hands kneading her breasts, while Philippa clutched at his jacket. Should she be doing something more? Part of her thought she should, but she could scarcely focus . . . not with the things *he* was doing to *her*. It was as though her body had been hibernating, and now spring had arrived and she was flush with new, overwhelming sensations, drowning in them.

When the kiss ended and he lowered his mouth to one of her throbbing nipples, she gasped and moaned, her head falling back against the seat, hands clutching at his hair.

"Oh my . . . oh Marcus . . . I . . ." She could not form a coherent sentence. Could not *think*.

"Shhh, Philippa." His teeth nipped gently, scraping across her nipple, and she whimpered. The sensations went straight through her to her core, which clenched in empty need. "Don't think. Just feel. I want to show you what a good friend I can be."

The darkly seductive chuckle that followed his statement was full of promise.

Don't think. Just feel.

She could do that.

Fabric rustled as his hands slid under her skirts,

pushing them up. Her skin tingled where he touched, his fingers gliding over her legs, parting them. In the dim light of the carriage, the sight of him ducking under her skirts was sinfully erotic. The sensation of his lips pressing against her inner thighs even more so.

He gripped her buttocks and pulled her forward so his mouth could reach her aching pussy, and Philippa cried out as his tongue slid into her wet, swollen folds. She quickly covered her mouth with her hand. Sheer erotic bliss filled her, her body rejoicing at the tender, expert touch of a man who knew exactly what he was doing . . . and who enjoyed doing it.

Clarence might have used his mouth, but he had never *feasted* upon her as Marcus was doing now. Had never devoured her. Had never taken his time to lick, lave, nibble, and measure every one of her reactions, so that he could return to the stimulation she liked best.

The rocking of the carriage, the audible sounds of people in the streets around them, and the heated interior all added to the illicitness of what Marcus was doing to her. His fingers dug into her buttocks, his tongue working across her flesh like he could not get enough of her taste, sliding inside of her and then slipping out to lick his way up to her clit again. Philippa began to feel quite light-headed, her hands tightening on his hair, the tension inside of her coiling and coiling until she could not contain it any longer.

It burst from her with a cry, and again she clapped one of her hands over her mouth, sure that someone must have heard, even if it was only the coachman. The urge to quiet herself was the only modest inclination left to her as she sat writhing on the seat, shuddering against

Marcus's tongue. She pressed him further between her legs, needing to eke out every last ounce of ecstasy her body could manage.

The hot suckling of her clit made her want to scream, and she just barely managed to clench her jaw against the sound of abject rapture. Tears slid down her cheeks as her months of abstinence were broken, the first true climax she'd had since before her husband's death wrecking her in the most lovely way possible.

Well, perhaps not *the* most lovely way. Her pussy still clenched emptily, aching to be filled, but in so many other ways she was satisfied in a manner she had not been able to achieve on her own.

Marcus's clever tongue lapped at her juices, and Philippa shuddered and jerked against the sensations, which were almost painfully pleasurable now after the peak of ecstasy. She panted in the hot carriage, the dim lighting making the moment seem surreal. And it was surreal, was it not? A man under her skirts, her breasts still bared, her body limp from pleasure . . .

The encounter had been so much more than she could have imagined. No wonder Clarence had had mistresses. For the first time, Philippa did not feel so badly that she had not been able to fulfill all of his needs. Certainly, if she had known the difference between a man like her husband, who had used his tongue rather conservatively, and a man like Marcus, who had clearly enjoyed putting his mouth to good use, she would have wanted both as well. Different lovers likely excelled at and enjoyed different things.

She did worry a bit as Marcus helped her put her dress back to rights. There was a prodigious bulge at the front of his breeches, but he made no further move toward her.

"Should I . . ." She nodded at his clearly erect cock, unsure as to how to phrase her question. "Would you . . ."

"Oh no, sweetheart," he said, lifting one hand to his lips to kiss. Even though he kissed the back of her hand, considering where his mouth had been just minutes earlier, there was a new intimacy to the gesture. "This was for you, remember? So you can consider the benefits of a . . . friendship with me. I certainly hope for one with you. I think it will be delicious." He flicked his tongue out and Philippa's body clenched.

Oh yes.

She did want that *friendship*. Would any woman in her right mind turn him down?

But since he seemed to want to give her time to think, she would wait to tell him so. Right now she felt too replete, too satisfied, to feel any urgency. Pulling the curtains back so that air could flow through the carriage again, Marcus smoothed his rumpled hair down as best he could and asked after her plans for the evening.

Far from being awkward, they found much to discuss on the remainder of the ride, leaving Philippa both pleased and relieved by the time the carriage pulled up in front of her house again. As Marcus helped her down, two gentlemen came walking up, and she immediately recognized Lord Sunderland and Lord Conyngham.

Seen together, they were clearly two of a sort—both attractive, well-dressed, but with an air about them that screamed "danger" to well-bred young ladies. Unlike Sunderland, Conyngham was looking at her with rakish intent and a knowing smirk that put a blush on her cheeks. Did he somehow know what she and Marcus had been doing in the carriage? Katherine had mentioned that Marcus had a reputation for that sort of thing, but Conyngham could not possibly *know* . . . could he?

"Lady Essex," Lord Sunderland greeted her, causing Marcus to turn. Sunderland took him in as well. "Mr. Horn."

"Sunderland. Conyngham." Marcus nodded at the two men. "Out for a stroll?"

"The weather is too fine not to," Conyngham said. "I would hate to miss any of the lovely sights the city has to offer." His gaze slid over to meet hers, and Philippa blinked in surprise at his implication.

It was no wonder he had such a reputation, he was very smooth and charming. And she was becoming quite the hussy, admiring one man while on the arm of another! But then, was that not the point of being a *merry* widow?

She did not have a rule book for this sort of thing, unfortunately.

"We do not want to keep you from your walk," Marcus said, smiling genially, but there was something in the air between him and the other man. Did Marcus know Conyngham was interested in her?

My, my, how times have changed, she reflected as she bid Sunderland and Conyngham farewell and let Marcus escort her to her door. From no man in her life at all, to multiple men pursuing her. Well, she assumed Conyngham was, but she did not think she had misread his intent.

Of course, she knew a rake like Conyngham would be interested in nothing more than seduction. Perhaps not even a *friendship* like Marcus. And that was just fine, she reminded herself. That was exactly what she wanted.

There was no reason at all to feel a bit empty inside.

CHAPTER SEVEN

"WE'RE NOT THE ONLY ONES AFTER LADY Essex."

Flicking his eyes up from his newspaper, Everett raised his eyebrow as Conyngham flopped into a chair beside him. "Of course we're not, did you think we would be?"

"Did you know she's already allowed Horn to sink his teeth into her?" Conyngham asked, somewhat irritably. Horn was well known among the rakes of the *ton* for his particular fetish—one which tended to make seduction harder for the rest of them. There was no formal competition among the rakes, but there was certainly an informal one, and Horn had a tendency to undercut those at the top of the heap, such as Everett and Conyngham.

Normally, Everett found it amusing.

Now, everything inside of him seized up, his throat tightening as if a noose had wrapped around it, making it hard for him to breathe.

A waiter appeared at Conyngham's shoulder, giving Everett a moment to compose himself before he needed to make a reply. Thankfully, White's was mostly empty at this time in the afternoon. The gentleman's club would soon be filling up for the dinner hour, but for now, he and Conyngham had this little corner of the room to themselves. Everett was especially thankful for Roger's absence.

By the time Conyngham ordered his drink, Everett had managed to wrest his emotions back under control. Mostly.

"You are certain things have progressed that far between them?" he asked, almost proud of how mild his tone was in comparison to how he felt.

Part of him had not truly believed Pippa's declaration.

He'd accepted that he would have to prove himself to her, and he'd been the one to set up the competition with Conyngham, but he had not expected her to truly be a *merry* widow. When they'd first met, she'd been so chaste and modest . . . but that had been before, and this was now.

Everett was certainly different from the callow youth she'd known. He hoped he'd improved. Sometimes he wondered though. . .

"Sunderland and I came upon them exiting Horn's carriage," Conyngham said with a reluctant sigh, tinged with admiration for Horn. "Horn's hair was rumpled, as were the skirts of her dress, and her cheeks were more flushed than a carriage ride could account for. I asked around and his carriage was seen traveling with the curtains drawn not long before that."

Jealousy churned Everett's insides, making him feel ill. He slumped back into the seat, doing his best to keep his emotions from his expression. Conyngham did not seem to notice anything amiss—he was too preoccupied with the arrival of his brandy. Everett took the opportunity to order another drink for himself.

Given this new revelation, fortification was required.

Still . . . perhaps he could use this to his advantage. Roger's words about the bet had not sat well with him, especially knowing he couldn't accurately predict Pippa's reactions and behaviors. She had never challenged him before. Except for the day when he'd told her about his parents' reaction to his desire to marry her.

It was clear he did not understand Pippa as well as he used to. As he'd thought he still would. Which meant that perhaps Roger was correct. Perhaps this bet was a poor idea.

"Should we have Sunderland find us another lady to settle our bet?" he asked casually, as if it did not matter to him either way.

He could then happily leave Conyngham to chase the new target and continue to pursue Pippa with Horn as his main competition. One plus to Horn being in that spot—many of the other rakes would cede him the field, at least for a while. Competition would be lower in general.

Unfortunately, after a moment of thought, Conyngham shook his head, a grin spreading across his face. "I cannot possibly run from a *greater* challenge; it will only make my inevitable triumph all the sweeter."

Everett scoffed, hiding his disappointment. "Inevitable only in your own mind."

"Have you even seen her?" Conyngham asked, almost taunting.

"The other night," Everett replied, accepting his new glass from the waiter. He took a sip, meeting Conyngham's eyes with a smirk. "We waltzed."

Conyngham scowled. "Where the bloody hell was she? I haven't seen her at any of the main events."

Rather than telling him that Pippa wasn't appearing at the main attractions each evening, Everett simply shrugged. "If you truly need my assistance . . ."

"Of course I don't." Conyngham sat back in his chair, the fingers of one hand drumming against the table, apparently lost in thought.

Eventually he would realize that he needed to accept the less prestigious invitations in order to find Pippa, but until he did Everett would use the one advantage he had.

Why was he persisiting in this bet . . . ?

If Sunderland had chosen a woman other than Pippa, and then Pippa had returned for the Season, Everett would not have bowed out either. He would have just allowed Conyngham to win while he pursued his own chosen lady. There was certainly no shame in losing to a practiced seducer like Conyngham. Their group was called *Rupert's* Rakes for a reason. But to quit the field entirely . . . to tell his friends why he did not want to compete with *Pippa* as a prize . . .

He would have to admit why he had changed his mind about the bet. Would have to confess his feelings. And then if she continued to spurn him, if he was unsuccessful in his courtship, he would not only be heartbroken, but his friends would all know of her rejection.

Perhaps he had not overcome his pride as much as he'd thought.

"How do I look?" Katherine appeared in Philippa's doorway, dressed in her finest day gown. The cheery yellow and mint jonquil fabric of her gown was at odds with her anxious expression, but she managed to look fetching nonetheless.

"Beautiful, of course," Philippa teased. "I told you when we bought the dress that it was perfect for you." Brightly colored, nipped in at the waist, and with a flattering neckline, it was the most expensive dress Katherine had allowed her to purchase that wasn't a ballgown. "I wager that *now* you are glad you let me buy it."

Katherine made a face at her. "I did not realize at the time that we'd be entertaining *dukes* or I would have insisted on a wardrobe of them."

It was a lie, as Katherine did not like for Philippa to "spoil" her, and they both knew it. Still, Philippa thought perhaps her companion was regretting not allowing Philippa to purchase a few more fancy dresses for her.

"Just one duke . . . so far," Philippa teased. "I sincerely doubt there will be more than one, for that matter."

The Duke of Beaufort was not a suitor anyhow. An old friend of her late husband, he had promised to assist her in any way after Clarence's death. Philippa had sometimes wished he had a wife for her to befriend, but he had never married and kept a longtime mistress instead. Of course, Philippa had never met the woman. She had always though the duke must truly love her in order to have stayed faithful to her all these years, never marrying despite the societal pressure to do so.

Philippa wondered why he did not just marry the mistress . . . she supposed the woman must be unsuitable in some way.

Her stomach twisted, the circumstances reminding her of how Hartington's parents had been horrified by the idea of his wife being the daughter of a *tradesman*. But surely, in his forties and already having inherited his title, Beaufort could do as he pleased.

Philippa pushed her thoughts away. It did not matter. Because she was not going to encourage Hartington's pursuit regardless. Whatever Beaufort's reason for not marrying, presuming he even wished to, it had no bearing on her situation with Hartington.

"Meeting one duke is more than enough," Katherine declared nervously, brushing imaginary lint from her skirt. Philippa laughed, but truthfully, she agreed. If she had not already met Beaufort before, she would certainly avoid him as much as she did any other duke.

Not that she was invited to the parties or balls where dukes would be found, so unless she ran into one on the street . . .

For a moment, she imagined wild dukes roaming the streets of London, popping out at random intervals to accost passersby with their dukely presence. She grinned, looking down at her jewelry so that Katherine did not see her expression and think Philippa was laughing at *her*.

Thankfully, when the Duke of Beaufort arrived, he was just as Philippa expected: charming, serious-minded, and very pleasant company all around. Katherine was able to relax when it was clear he did not mind an intelligent woman—indeed, they started discussing some of the recent scientific discoveries being made in Germany, and the conversation left Philippa quite in the dust.

"Oh, I'm so sorry, Philippa," Katherine said, looking contrite when the soup course ended and both she and the duke seemed to realize together that Philippa had not said a word the whole time. "I know you are not as interested in these motor engines as I am."

Philippa smiled at her friend. "I'm afraid I just do not see the point of them. Our entire society is built around horses and carriages—not some mechanical machinery that sounds as though it is constantly falling apart."

"But if it *stopped* falling apart . . ." Katherine started to enthuse and then caught herself, her eyes twinkling merrily. She shook her head. "But we should discuss something you will enjoy as well."

"I have been entertained hearing the two of you enjoy yourselves," Philippa said immediately, flashing both of them a smile. "Is that not the duty of a good hostess?"

"You have always been an exemplary hostess," Beaufort said, tilting his head toward her. There was a slightly odd expression on his face, one that Philippa had not seen before and could not decipher. "However, I was wondering if you might allow me to host you next. I have decided to retreat from London next Thursday and am inviting others to join me at Bellham Hall. I would be most pleased if you ladies joined us." He smiled at Katherine. "I think you will find quite a few topics to your interest among my guests."

Which meant Philippa might not, but seeing the way Katherine brightened with hope, she could hardly say no. After all, Katherine accompanied her to teas and various balls almost daily, which were certainly not her preferred entertainment.

"We would be happy to, thank you, your grace," Philippa answered immediately, and Beaufort turned his attention back to her with a pleased smile.

"I know it is not always fashionable to leave London at the height of the Season, but . . ." He shrugged, clearly not caring what was or was not fashionable. Then he smiled again. "I will invite your friend Lady Hertford and her husband as well, of course."

Philippa could only smile. He likely worried about what she and Katherine might be missing by stepping away from the city for a weekend. She was unbothered. While she enjoyed the events she attended, she also found them wearing. Especially knowing that Hartington was now in pursuit of her. An escape from the city next week might be very welcome.

"That is very kind of you, thank you." She wasn't surprised he knew that she rarely attended any events without Olivia, although she doubted he realized how many invitations Olivia turned down because Philippa's presence was unwelcome there. Philippa felt a great deal of guilt over it, even though Olivia swore she was happier this way.

Apparently, the *ton* had not forgotten that she came from trade, her new status as a dowager countess notwithstanding. Attending a duke's house party could only increase her social standing, which might benefit Olivia in the latter part of the Season. Truthfully, she could think of no good reason to say no, and quite a few reasons to say yes.

When the doorbell rang that afternoon, both Katherine and Philippa looked up at each other and frowned. For once, they were taking an afternoon off of social activities, as she had been uncertain how long Beaufort would stay after lunch. As it happened, he'd had a prior social engagement, leaving them with several hours to themselves. Neither of them were upset about the unexpected windfall.

Katherine had already ensconced herself on a window seat with the most recently printed *Intellectual Observer* while Philippa was settled in her favorite armchair with the much less intellectually edifying (but much more entertaining to her) penny romance.

"I take it you did not expect another visitor?" Katherine asked after seeing Philippa's confusion.

"No." Anxiety rose immediately. Was it Hartington? Her heart began to pound. Did she *want* it to be Hartington?

Technically, she and Katherine were not at home, so Thomas, her butler, should send whoever it was away. Unless, of course, they were high ranking enough that he felt his duty was to give her the choice to send them away. Such as the son of a duke.

Footsteps began to come down the hall. Blast! It had to be Hartington. Anticipation curled with tension in her stomach, an unholy mix that did nothing to help her emotional state. By the time Thomas appeared in the doorway to the parlor, as stiffly upright as ever, she still did not know how she was going to respond.

"My lady, the Earl of Conyngham wishes to know if you are receiving."

Philippa blinked.

Conyngham.

Disappointment and relief rose inside of her in equal measure, and she internally cursed her confused emotions. She shouldn't be disappointed. Which was what pushed her into accepting the earl's call. Otherwise, she doubted she would be able to focus on the story she was reading; she would just sit and think about why she was disappointed it had not been Hartington calling.

Standing, she set down her periodical and brushed her skirts off. "I will receive him in the drawing room. Ask Mrs. Pound to send in some tea and biscuits."

Thomas nodded and left, and Katherine stood as well, looking confused. "Do you want me to come?"

"I . . ." The truth was, she did. She did not know anything about Conyngham, and having Katherine there would make her more comfortable, but she also felt guilty about accepting his call without first discussing it with her companion.

As soon as she hesitated, Katherine put down her *Observer* and stood as well. "I am coming."

"Thank you," Philippa said with relief. She still felt a tinge of guilt, but hopefully whatever Conyngham wanted would not take long.

By the time they reached the drawing room, Conyngham was already there, peering out of the window into the gardens. When she and Katherine entered, he straightened with a smile that only slipped slightly when he saw she wasn't alone.

"My lady," he said with a bow.

"My lord," she curtseyed. "May I introduce you to my companion, Katherine Parrish. Katherine, the Earl of Conyngham."

"Charmed," he said, coming to bow over Katherine's hand and giving her a wink. To Philippa's surprise, Katherine actually blushed. But then, Conyngham was a force of nature.

Today he looked even more devastatingly handsome than he had on the street; he was dressed to impress, hazel eyes alight charming intent. He turned those eyes on Philippa the moment he dropped Katherine's hand.

"You are a hard woman to track down, my lady." The almost lazy smile that crossed his lips was really quite attractive, as it revealed the dimples in his cheeks. "I am sorry I missed your at-home, but I appreciate you opening your door to me this afternoon."

"Pure curiosity," she admitted, sitting down on the chaise with Katherine and leaving the chair for Conyngham. He sat down in an elegant slouch. Philippa was impressed—he somehow managed to look both completely relaxed and yet like he could spring to action at any moment. In some ways, he reminded her of how she'd always pictured a lion. "I could not imagine what might bring you to my doorstep."

"I prefer the doorsteps of beautiful ladies," he responded, making Katherine blush again. Both women stared at him, slightly shocked at his brazen statement. Then again, he was a rake, wasn't he? It was flattering, to say the least, and Philippa rather admired his boldness.

"Do you visit many of them?" she asked, meeting his boldness with her own. Katherine let out a tiny squeak, which only Philippa heard. She was certain her companion would be giving her quite the lecture once they were alone again.

"Now and then." He winked again, his smile turning rather wicked, and now Philippa felt like blushing as well. There was just something about the way he looked at her that made her feel, well, *naked*. In an enjoyable but not entirely comfortable way. "It *has* been a while since I visited two at once."

Philippa's cheeks now felt like they were burning, and this time Katherine's squeak was entirely audible. Conyngham's smile widened as Katherine jumped to her feet. "I'll . . . I . . . I'm going to go check on the tea."

With that, Philippa's companion fled, leaving her alone with the rake.

Philippa did not blame Katherine for her retreat. After all, Philippa had been encouraging him; Katherine likely thought she was doing Philippa a favor, as well as giving herself time to recover her sensibilities.

But Philippa did not actually know what to do with a true rake either. She was wildly out of her depth.

And she was very much afraid that Conyngham knew it.

CHAPTER EIGHT

WITH KATHERINE'S DEPARTURE, THE ATMOS-
phere in the room somehow intensified. Conyngham's
attention was no longer divided; instead it was focused
entirely on her. She was beginning to feel like a mouse
caught in a trap with a cat . . . except that she did not
entirely hate being there.

*If he were Mr. Horn, he would want to eat me in a
different manner.*

The thought nearly made her burst out laughing, but
she managed to suppress the sound. Instead, she smiled
widely, and Conyngham's smile widened in return.
Triumph tinged his expression, and he got to his feet and
stepped forward . . . stepped toward her, eyes on her lips.
Like he was going to kiss her.

Heart pounding, Philippa jumped to her feet as well,
side stepping away from him. "Would you like to tour the
garden?" she blurted out.

Coming to an abrupt halt, Conyngham blinked, as if
processing her request.

It wasn't that she was averse to beginning a new *friendship*—assuming Conyngham wanted more than a single

encounter—but she did not know him at all. No matter how attractive he was, Philippa did not feel comfortable enough to allow him to kiss her on the basis of one dance and a short conversation in the street.

That he seemed to want her was very flattering, but she did not know whether she wanted *him*.

On the other hand, another gentleman caller—a clear rake—might also help deter Hartington.

"I would love a tour of the garden," Conyngham said, clearly undeterred by her sudden wavering. He offered up his arm, and Philippa realized her mistake. She gave him a look as she took the proffered arm, to which he winked in response, but he did not make a move to further intimacies.

Instead, he let her lead him out into the garden.

To her surprise, not only did he not make a move to kiss her again the entire time they were walking along the paths, but he was quite knowledgeable about flowers as well. The conversation was lively and engaging, and by the time they returned to the house, Philippa was much more relaxed in his presence—which was very likely the point.

It wasn't until they entered the room laughing, and Katherine looked up from her seat on the couch, that Philippa even remembered her earlier wariness. Within half an hour, he had set Katherine at ease too, charming her as easily and thoroughly as he had Philippa.

Oh yes, the Earl of Conyngham was a dangerous man indeed.

When it was time for him to leave, he bowed over her and Katherine's hands again.

"May I ask where you intend to spend your evening?"

He smiled roguishly at her. "So I do not have to spend *mine* traversing from house to house, and still come up empty."

Philippa laughed. He must be teasing, but she was still amused at the idea of an earl searching through the events of the *ton* just to find her. "We will be at Berkshire House this evening."

Surprise showed on his face only for a moment, and Philippa sighed inwardly. The Baron and Baroness of Berkshire were very kind people, but she was well aware theirs was not the premiere event of the evening. She would have gone nonetheless, because she truly liked them, but there were much larger gatherings to which she had not been invited. It hurt to know she was still unwelcome in the *ton*, just because her father was in trade.

The dwindling invitations were also more proof that Hartington could not possibly marry her. She'd turned into more of a social leper than she had been before. If the house party at the Duke of Beaufort's estate did not help her social status, she might give up entirely. Olivia would not want to abandon her, but her friend deserved to shine, and it had become entirely clear that the scandalous beginning of Olivia's marriage had already been forgotten, whereas Philippa's tainted dowry had not.

"Then I will see you at Berkshire House," Conyngham said smoothly, covering his initial reaction.

Philippa raised her eyebrows. "Do you have an invitation?"

She thought it most unlikely that the baron and baroness would have invited such a lofty presence. Especially on a night when there were several other major events. They had cheerfully told her that they preferred to entertain on such nights, so they could socialize without having to deal with a complete crush. They were happy hosts, not ambitious ones.

"I am the Earl of Conyngham," he said, drawing himself up haughtily, the twinkle in his eye belying his sudden airs. "I can guarantee I will be received."

Katherine giggled and Philippa just shook her head, not even trying to hide her smile. He was likely right. It wasn't as if the baroness would turn him away, even without an invitation.

"Then I shall look for you," she promised.

"And save me a dance."

"And save you a dance."

Bemused, she and Katherine watched him go. Then Katherine turned to her, tilting her head in question.

"So? Are you going to have two lovers?"

"I suppose it depends," Philippa said slowly. She tapped her finger against her lips. "He did seem very keen, did he not?"

"Very handsome, as well."

"Very."

"He would likely make Everett extremely jealous."

"Ye—" Philippa caught herself before agreeing. Her heart belatedly skipped a beat. She did not even refer to Hartington by his Christian name in her head. Meeting Katherine's eyes, she glared, but only for a moment before she sighed. "I do not want him *jealous*. I just want . . ."

Her voice trailed off.

In truth, she wanted him to writhe with jealousy and witness everything he'd lost when he'd thrown her away.

She wanted him to be telling the truth about still wanting to marry her.

She wanted him to leave her alone.

But of those three options, only one of them had the potential to break her heart. She did not even know why she wanted it. They were not the same people they had been. She had been wedded and widowed and he . . . he had turned into an unrepentant rake. No, she would be a fool to believe him and a fool to stake her hopes on him again.

"I want him to leave me be," she said harshly, turning and marching to the stairs.

She had a ball to get ready for.

Conyngham came to call while Everett was dressing for the evening, which was unusual enough that he told the butler to send the earl straight in. There must be something in the wind for Conyngham to come to him at home rather than seeking him out this evening. Not that Conyngham would be likely to find him, where Everett was going.

Except, apparently Conyngham would be, because the first words out of his mouth when he barged into Everett's room were, "Did you know she was going to be at Berkshire House this evening?"

Inwardly, he sighed. It seemed Conyngham had figured out his own way to find Philippa. Hopefully not the same chatty maid whom Everett's footman had made time with. She'd been happy to gossip about her mistress's goings-on, including the Duke of Beaufort's house party that they'd be attending next weekend. Everett was already making his own plans to secure an invitation, and he'd rather not spend the time competing with Conyngham for her attention.

"I did," he confirmed. Which meant he'd be competing with Conyngham for her attention this evening.

"Did you know she has not attended *any* of the major events this Season?" Conyngham asked. Frowning, Everett abandoned his effort to make the waterfall knot in his cravat and turned to look at his friend. He sounded almost distressed.

"Yes," Everett said slowly. Obviously the question meant something to Conyngham, but Everett could not think what. They stared at each other for a long moment and then Conyngham shook his head.

"You don't know."

"Know what?" Everett was beginning to become frustrated by this baffling line of conversation. He was pulled back by the grim look in Conyngham's eyes.

"Did you ever think to question *why* she has not been at any of the major events?"

Had he? Not really. Everett hardly kept up with what the major events were—and he did not much like attending them either. It made sense to him that Philippa would want a quiet Season her first Season back. Especially since she was doing the rounds with Olivia, for *her* first Season following her scandalous marriage.

But clearly Conyngham thought there was something more.

"Why?" he asked, rather than play Conyngham's guessing game.

"Unlike you, that's exactly what I asked myself," Conyngham said, pacing over to the window and staring out moodily at the landscape. Everett suppressed the urge to strangle his friend. Conyngham could sometimes take forever to get to the point of a story. He would get there eventually though, and he would do so faster if allowed to tell it in his own manner. "I thought of several reasons, but none which quite seemed to fit her now that I've gotten to know her a little better."

"You have?" That drew Everett's attention much more than Conyngham's monologuing.

Conyngham barely glanced at him. "This afternoon, I called and she gave me a tour of the garden before we had tea. She's delightful." The sincere admiration in his voice stirred Everett's jealousy. He already knew Pippa was delightful, but he did not like the idea of her being delightful with a man he knew planned to seduce her. "Smart, charming, clearly enjoys being social . . . so why has she been so hard to find? It made no sense. So I went to my mother."

Of course he had. His mother was one of the most prolific gossips of the *ton* and she was always happy to share whatever she knew with everyone she knew. If her son were asking after a particular lady, she'd likely even go and find more information for him.

Turning away from the window, Conyngham pinned Everett with a stern stare. He froze, unused to having such antagonism directed at him, especially from someone as easygoing as Conyngham. "My mother said that *your* mother has made it clear that Lady Essex is not good company. In fact, that she would not be seen at any house in which Lady Essex has been a guest."

Rage rose up inside of Everett, choking him. His mother did not even know that Everett was in pursuit of Pippa again, but she was doing her best to ruin Pippa socially anyway. He did not doubt Conyngham for one moment. While the countess might be a gossip, if she said something factually, it was because she'd heard it herself.

"You truly did not know," Conyngham murmured, sounding relieved. The angry glare he'd directed at Everett faded, but only a little. "*Why* does your mother have such a vendetta against Lady Essex?"

Turning away from the all-too-astute hazel eyes, Everett rubbed his chin. He did not want to admit the whole story . . . but he had to tell Conyngham something.

"Lady Essex and I knew each other before she was Lady Essex," he said finally. "My mother did not approve, and our acquaintance ended before she was married."

There was so much left out of the explanation, but Conyngham accepted it with a snort. "Does your mother approve of anyone?"

Everett winced. "Trust me, you do not want to meet the ladies my mother approves of." They tended to be just like her, but younger and more malleable. Just as haughty, just as snobbish about their social position, but, unlike his mother, willing to be led. She wanted him to marry someone just like her, but whom she could control.

He could not imagine anything more horrifying.

"Can you do anything to rein her in?" Conyngham inquired, looking thoughtful. "My mother said there are few who are willing to go against your mother's wishes, but Lady Essex deserves better."

Could he? Doubtful. But Conyngham was correct about what Pippa deserved. He could scarcely believe his mother was still holding a grudge, about a woman who had married someone else nonetheless. It did not bode well for a future with both Pippa and his parents, but this time if he had to choose, his mother would not like the end result.

"I can try." He sighed again and then brightened. "On

the other hand, who do you think the *ton* will care about more? My mother, or entire groups of young men?"

Because if Rupert's Rakes suddenly disappeared from the social scene, it would immediately be noticed. Most likely, it would first be noticed by the other young men, who would want to know why and where they had gone. They would go looking for the rakes, and then the young ladies and their matchmaking mamas would follow. If it became clear that they appeared if and only if Lady Essex was there, well . . .

"That is positively Machiavellian," Conyngham said after a moment, his expression lightening. "It will not do your mother any good to dig in her heels—she can only control the hostesses, not everyone else."

Everett wouldn't put it past her to try, but when it came down to it, matchmaking was what drove the Season. And to make matches, there needed to be gentlemen. He gave up on his cravat entirely, setting it down and moving to the door.

"Come on," he said grimly, jerking his head at Conyngham. "She's going to be at the Farthingale's ball tomorrow. Let's rally the troops."

Nodding his agreement, Conyngham followed Everett to his study, where they could send out notes to all of their friends—not just the rakes. He'd be late to Berkshire House, and he'd have to share Pippa tomorrow with an overabundance of other gentlemen, but Conyngham was correct. She deserved better.

If it meant adding to his competition for her attention, so be it.

CHAPTER NINE

"HE'S HERE!"

Philippa's distraction was such that she did not immediately know who Olivia was urgently whispering into
her ear about—Hartington or Conyngham. She'd been
nervously awaiting the appearance of either for what felt
like hours. Not that Hartington had said he would be
there, but she felt he would not have given up his pursuit
so soon or so easily.

She'd hoped that Conyngham would already be there
as a buffer, if and when Hartington did arrive, but he had
also yet to appear.

Head jerking around, she was surprised to realize
Olivia's whisper could refer to either of them. Both had
just entered the ballroom. Conyngham, with Sunderland
again, was walking several steps ahead of Hartington
and another man. It only took Philippa a few moments
to realize the other man was Roger Hervey, Hartington's
best friend, whom she'd met on many occasions *before*.
He looked more confident than he had when she'd known
him, more rakish.

Their entrance had caused a small stir all around the

ballroom, and the baron and baroness hurried forward to greet them. The men were so delayed that the receiving line had ended, but personages of their stature could not go without some kind of reception from the hosts. Even if they had not been invited.

"My goodness," Olivia murmured, fanning herself as she took in the sight. "If I did not have Francis to go home to . . ."

Philippa elbowed her. "Rakes are how you ended up married to Francis in the first place," she whispered back.

Not that Francis was a rake. No, he'd been a gentleman willing to step up when Olivia had fallen in with a rake— one who had fled the scene when they'd been caught kissing with his hand up her skirt, leaving Olivia's reputation in tatters. Francis had wanted to marry her anyway, helping to sweep the scandal under the rug.

"True enough, and . . . oh my, they are all headed this way!" Olivia's fan fluttered faster. "Do you think they are *all* here for you?"

"Certainly not," Philippa said immediately. In fact, when Hervey spotted her, his expression was more resigned than anything else. He, at least, was not overjoyed to see her. Hartington, by contrast, brightened and then began forging his way through the crowd with sheer determination on his face, Conyngham not far behind.

"Two of them are, at least," Olivia observed, eyeing Philippa with a touch of concern.

Philippa did not know how to feel. She was flattered and intrigued to see Conyngham, but that paled in comparison to the bundle of nerves, excitement, dread, and the awful spark of hope that Hartington engendered inside of her. Turning away, she pretended she had not noticed them, taking a moment to gather herself.

With Olivia on her right, and Katherine quickly sidling up to her left the moment she assessed the situation, Philippa was able to breathe a small sigh of relief. Her friends were there to bolster her, and they did not even know about Hartington's declaration yet. She had not been able to bring herself to speak of it, not even to her two closest friends.

That was probably going to have to change after tonight.

Joining forces with Conyngham had been necessary, but Everett wished it had not been. While Conyngham easily found a place beside Pippa in her circle, *he* found himself being consistently thwarted by the Marchioness of Hertford and Pippa's companion, Miss Parrish. Both of them looked at him with suspicion and hostility in their eyes, although they remained civil.

Grimacing, Everett looked to Roger for help, but his friend was speaking with another gentleman who made up part of Pippa's circle, a Mr. Martin, and did not catch his eye. Desperate, he turned his silent plea to Sunderland as well, whose lips twitched with amusement. Sunderland could not know exactly what was going on, or why Pippa's friends were so eager to keep him from her, but he clearly saw that Conyngham currently had the advantage.

Thankfully, he gallantly stepped forward as the violins tested a few notes, stopping in front of Miss Parrish. The young woman, who was rather pretty if not the stunner that the marchioness and Pippa were, blinked in surprise.

"Miss Parrish, would you do me the honor of a dance?" Sunderland asked, holding out his hand.

She blinked again, her mouth opening and then closing, her expression conflicted.

Beside her, Pippa looked delighted. "Oh yes, Katherine, you do love to dance, and you hardly ever do."

Miss Parrish muttered something under her breath at her mistress, but then she turned and smiled at Sunderland as she took his hand. "Yes, thank you, my lord."

One protector down, one to go. Everett and the marchioness eyed each other. The soft brown eyes she was known for—one poet had compared them to a doe's—were hard as granite when he met them. If Everett was going to make any headway with Pippa, he was going to have to persuade the marchioness that he meant no harm.

Which would likely be difficult. Back when she had been Lady Olivia, before her marriage, she and Pippa had been bosom friends . . . and she clearly knew how to hold a grudge.

"My lady," he said with a bow, startling both the marchioness and Pippa as he bowed to the former rather than the latter. "Would you do me the honor of a dance?"

Despite how his rank had hindered his and Pippa's relationship the first time round, now it was one of his greatest assets, at least when it came to the social arena. The marchioness knew it too. Such a polite request would cause more trouble if refused than accepted.

"Very well," she said, much less graciously than Miss Parrish had accepted Sunderland's invitation. Despite her waspishness, Everett could not suppress a smile. He did not begrudge Pippa such protective friends. If he could win them to *his* side as well, it would be a major victory.

Joining Sunderland and Miss Parrish on the dance floor, he was unsurprised and resigned when Conyngham and Pippa followed as well. He'd expected it, but he still did not *like* it.

Settling into position for the waltz, he looked down at the marchioness, who pursed her lips and glared up at him.

"What do you want, Hartington?" she asked, as forward as when she was a debutante. He'd always liked that about her. It certainly made negotiations easier.

"I want a dance with Pippa."

The marchioness narrowed her eyes at him. "*Lady Capell.*"

He gritted his teeth. "Lady Capell."

Using her married name made his teeth ache. Not just his teeth. His chest. His heart. But he did it, to placate the marchioness. He'd be willing to do much worse if it meant dancing with Pippa tonight.

"I did not mean tonight," the marchioness said sternly. The woman could give any old dragon of the *ton* a run for their money when it came to the evil eye. "What do you *want* with her?"

"I want to marry her."

She laughed in his face. She laughed so hard that she snorted and nearly tripped over his feet, and yet kept laughing because she could not seem to stop.

Definitely not encouraging. Everett's heart sank in his chest. Almost gasping for air, she managed to wrest control over herself and peered up at him. "My god . . . you're in earnest. Why on earth do you think she'd be willing to put herself through that again?"

"It's different this time. This time my parents have no more power over me." His jaw felt strained from the clenching muscles. "I do not care if they cut me off. I am not dependent on them anymore."

"You risk social ruin, if your mother has her way." The marchioness's eyes glinted with anger. *She* knew the hand his mother had to play in Pippa's current social situation. Everett wondered if Pippa did as well. He hoped not. He did not need any other points against him in her mind.

"I have had Society for the past two years," he said grimly. "I would rather have Pippa. And Conyngham and I have a plan. She should begin receiving invitations within a fortnight."

The marchioness gave him a skeptical look, but focused on his first statement rather than the second. "*Lady Capell* has no wish to marry again."

"She was very clear how she felt about my suit," Everett said dryly. "Nonetheless, I am going to try. No matter how you and Miss Parrish maneuver to block me, I will still try."

Something in the marchioness's expression changed, and she glanced over to where Conyngham and Pippa were twirling about the floor. Pippa laughed at something Conyngham said, and Everett's stomach churned with jealous worry.

"You told her . . ." the marchioness murmured.

"I told her I wish to marry her," he replied, and then realized, "she did not tell *you?*"

"No, she did not," she confirmed, pursing her lips thoughtfully. "I do not know what that means."

Neither did he.

The notes of the song were coming to a close, and he looked down at the marchioness, letting his plea show on his face. "Tonight, I just wish a dance with her."

With a heavy sigh, the marchioness nodded. Then a small smile curved her lips. "It will be her punishment for keeping things from me."

Wonderful. Dancing with him as a punishment. Now it was Everett's turn to sigh. The marchioness smirked at him.

The expression on Olivia's face when she returned to their circle had Philippa wondering exactly what Hartington had said to her. There was no way to find out until later, though.

Conversations struck up again, but this time Olivia let Hartington take her place next to Philippa. She shot her friend a look. Olivia sent the look right back, further rousing Philippa's curiosity as to what exactly Hartington had said to her during their dance. Whatever it was, she apparently had lost one of her guard dogs.

On her other side, Katherine was fully distracted by Lord Sunderland. It almost sounded like the two of them were arguing over something, but Philippa could tell Katherine was enjoying herself. She only argued with those she thought were worth the time to do so. That Sunderland seemed just as invigorated was very interesting.

Philippa had encouraged Katherine to dance with him because her companion was so seldom asked to, and she did love to dance. She had not thought anything other than a dance would actually come from it, but apparently Sunderland's demeanor toward Katherine had changed substantially during the course of it.

Of course, without her two protectors, she could not avoid a dance with Hartington when he asked.

The moment he put his hand on her waist, her entire body felt like it seized up. Philippa put it down to the history between them. She was attracted to other men.

Interested in them, even. That her body responded so strongly to Hartington was inconsequential.

"Very fine weather we're having," she commented, at a loss of what else she could possibly say. Lack of conversation would have grated on her just as badly.

Hartington chuckled. "Really Pippa?"

"Stop calling me that," she snapped back. "I go by Philippa now."

"Philippa then." He said her name like he was tasting it for the first time, and there was a flash of triumph in his eyes.

"Lady Essex to you," she said coldly.

"No, no, you just said Philippa." He shook his head. "Let us not go backward in our friendship. You are Philippa now and you may call me Everett."

"We don't *have* a friendship," she hissed at him. He spun her round another couple and she nearly stepped on his foot. By instinct, she avoided doing so, and then immediately wished she *had* trod on him. He would have deserved it.

Looking thoughtful, he nodded. "You are right. What's between us is so much more."

Her breath caught in her throat when he looked down at her, and for one shining moment she was two years younger, staring up at the man she loved while he gazed adoringly at her, and the whole world was at her feet. Some part of her yearned to be that girl again, even as the older, wiser version of herself balked.

"No," she said, shaking her head firmly. "No, no, no, no, *no*."

Not caring about the gossip, not caring about the scandal, she pulled away from him and left him there in the middle of the dance floor. She fled back to Katherine and Olivia. They came to her sides instantly, shields against the bystanders. Shields against Hartington. Against herself.

Because the temptation to believe him, to put her trust in him, had been kindled inside of her. She *had* to snuff it out before she faced him again. Certainly dancing with him was far too dangerous to her emotions. Too many memories. Too intimate.

"I have a *megrim*," she said, putting her hand to her head. At least, she could feel one gathering, so it was not entirely a lie. Neither Olivia nor Katherine protested; instead, they bustled her out of the house so quickly that she barely had time to catch her breath before she was in the carriage and safely away.

Well, she had thought she was safe until Olivia spoke up.

"So." Olivia tilted her head in question. Even in the darkness of the carriage, Philippa could see the sharp look in her eye. "Hartington told me he proposed to you again."

"He *what?*" Katherine shrieked, sitting straight up in shock.

Philippa groaned. She should have just stayed home tonight.

It was not the most successful evening he'd ever had, but Everett did not consider it completely *un*successful either. Some might. Conyngham had practically crowed when Pippa left in the middle of her dance with Everett, hounding Everett to ask what he had said that had sent her running.

Thankfully, Conyngham had assumed Everett had hit on a sore subject or somehow otherwise, unknowingly, insulted her. He had missed the expression on Pippa's face just before she'd run. Only Everett had been close enough to see it.

She'd been looking up at him the way she had *before*. And then she'd run.

Not from *him*, although that's what Conyngham assumed, but from herself. From her feelings for him. They might be buried deep, they might be unwanted, but they were still there.

Now at home, sitting back in his favorite chair, smoking his pipe, Everett smiled into the darkness. There was hope.

CHAPTER TEN

THERE WERE SEVERAL DRAWBACKS TO rallying the troops to support Pippa.

The very next night, when all of Rupert's Rakes and nearly a dozen other gentlemen and lords descended on the Farthingale's ball, all of them were in hot pursuit of Pippa. The Rakes were happy to watch Conyngham and Everett compete for her attentions, but the others were more interested in the woman herself.

Since Pippa was now even warier of him than before, she was able to use those gentlemen as a shield against him. Not only that, but the Marquess of Hertford had joined his wife, giving her another source of support. The marchioness, while no longer outwardly hostile, seemed to take great amusement at Everett's frustration.

The night after the Farthingale's ball, more gentlemen joined them at Shannesty House. Then Lady Massey's Masquerade. Then the Marchioness of Hertford sent him a note. Pippa had been invited to Lady Marchmont's ball—a premier event to which she had not previously received an invitation. Several other invitations had followed, all with apologies for their tardy arrival. The marchioness thanked him for his efforts in counteracting the *ton*'s antipathy toward Pippa, by which she actually meant his mother's vendetta.

The *ton* had spoken—where the gentlemen congregated was more important than the presence of one duchess. Even though it was the marchioness thanking him instead of Pippa, Everett still felt a swell of triumph.

It was progress.

And, as far as he knew, no one else knew that she would soon be retreating from London for the Duke of Beaufort's house party. He'd managed to secure an invitation by calling upon the duke under the guise of a bill coming up in the House of Lords and then confiding in the older man that he was feeling fatigued by the Season. A considerate gentleman, Beaufort had immediately spoken of his house party and told Everett he would be welcome. Of course, Everett had happily accepted.

Even if Pippa was managing to avoid him now, it would be much more difficult at a house party. In the meantime, he sent her flowers daily, always expressing his continuing love and devotion. Whether or not they made any difference, he had no idea, but at least he felt as though he was doing something.

Staring at the latest of Hartington's bouquets—this one large enough that Katherine was almost completely hidden behind it as she circled around to take in the arrangement in all its glory—Philippa had no idea what to do.

"Do you think he will keep making them larger and larger until you send him a response?" Katherine asked, echoing the thought Philippa was currently having. It certainly seemed that might be his goal. This monstrosity must have cost him a fortune.

"Do you think I should?" she asked, a bit plaintively. Truthfully, she did not trust any of her reactions.

If she sent him a note, was it truly because she wanted him to stop sending flowers, or because she craved some kind of communication with him?

If she did *not* send him a note, did it truly mean she did not care, or was it really because some part of her enjoyed having increasingly decadent arrangements appearing daily?

If she did write him a note, and the flower deliveries ceased, how would she feel?

Every direction seemed mired with hidden traps for her conflicted emotions. That she was conflicted at all only served to make her both angrier and warier. How could she possibly be thinking of giving him another chance?

Yet, every night, despite the gentlemen crowding around her, despite how she avoided and ignored him as much as possible, there he was. And the next day she'd receive another bouquet of flowers, declaring his feelings and intentions. Olivia had already softened toward him, and now it seemed Katherine might be softening as well. Philippa did not know how she felt.

"Between his offerings and the other gentlemen, your parlor is beginning to resemble a conservatory," Katherine observed, rather than answering Philippa's question. That she didn't respond with a resounding "no" was an answer in and of itself.

"I think Olivia thinks he has something to do with our sudden influx of invitations," Philippa murmured. Her friend had hinted as such the night before, and ever since the invitations had begun to arrive, Olivia had not said one harsh word about Hartington.

Philippa did not know how to feel about the invitations any more than she did about Hartington. While she was glad to no longer be a social albatross, hanging round Olivia's neck, she hated being in debt to him. She wanted to thumb her nose at all the lords and ladies who had not initially welcomed her presence, but she was also pragmatic enough to know that was how Society worked.

"He and Conyngham," Katherine confirmed, surprising Philippa. She shot her friend a questioning look and, to her surprise, Katherine colored a delicate pink and avoided meeting her eyes. "Lord Sunderland told me."

"Oh really?" Philippa asked, not bothering to hide her delight. While Sunderland had continued to spend time with Katherine each evening, she had not realized things had grown so serious. Katherine had not said much more than that he had an astute mind and was a good conversationalist; but apparently they were exchanging more than intellectual observations.

Shrugging, Katherine did her best to look diffident, but the blush remained stubbornly on her cheeks. "He mentioned it when I told him we may soon be attending more than one event an evening. He said Conyngham and Hartington both felt you deserved better than how the *ton* was treating you, and so they called in their friends to accompany them as they followed you about town."

After which point, even more gentlemen had followed. No wonder she was beset with suitors. Half of them were most likely only interested because Conyngham and Hartington were. Although she could not yet determine *how* interested Conyngham was. With the increase in competition for her attention, he had not been able to get her alone again. She did not know whether to be relieved or disappointed.

While she very much enjoyed his company, there was also a stubborn part of her that disliked the idea of being the lover of one of Hartington's friends. They were friends, too, she had realized over the past few nights. Rivals, yes, but also friends. It made the whole situation so much more complicated.

"Perhaps you should wait to respond until after Mr. Horn comes for tea tomorrow," Katherine suggested. "You might be more clearheaded about how you want to proceed afterwards."

Yes, because Marcus was coming to . . . further their friendship. At least, that was Philippa's understanding. She was nervous, excited, and yet, part of her felt a tinge of guilt. As if she were being unfaithful to Hartington.

Which was ridiculous. They were not together. She had promised him nothing. And back when they had made promises to each other, *he* had been the one to break faith. Philippa pursed her lips. Yes. She would review her options again tomorrow, *after* Marcus's visit.

Light came crashing through his room, along with the sound of curtains being hastily thrown open, and Everett awoke with a strangled shout. It was far too early for Hendricks to wake him, and his valet never did so by opening the curtains so abruptly.

"What in the blazes—" He cut off the question when his exhausted eyes took in the sight of his mother standing at the foot of his bed, fists pressed on her hips, her expression filled with disapproval. He yanked his sheets back up over his bare chest.

"My apologies, my lord," Hendricks's voice came from the direction of the door, but Everett kept his gaze on his mother rather than look at his extremely apologetic valet. "She refused to wait—"

"I should not have to wait to see my son." The sharp remark was directed at Everett. She would blame him for his staff trying to do their job, when she was the one who had shown up uninvited and without warning, far earlier in the day than any decent person would.

Since she herself was not fond of early mornings, Everett knew that whatever had brought her here in such a state would not make for enjoyable conversation. Still, if he was going to have to face the dragon, he should at least be dressed and fed. Coffee would not go amiss either.

"Waiting until I am at least awake would have been polite," he chided her, but the attempt was useless. His mother was completely inured to criticism.

"You are awake now."

Everett gritted his teeth, praying for patience. "So I am. Very well. If you will follow Hendricks to the dining room, I will be along momentarily, and we can discuss whatever brings you here at this ungodly hour of the morning over breakfast."

His mother narrowed her eyes at him, and for a moment he thought she would refuse and insist on having the discussion while he was still sitting in his bed, but fortunately she nodded and turned to stride out the door. "I know my way to the dining room. Hendricks can stay here to help you dress. Do not dawdle."

Groaning, Everett flopped back onto his bed, flinging his arm over his eyes as soon as she had left the room.

"I am sorry, my lord," Hendricks said, his voice coming closer, full of contrition. "None of us knew how to stop her."

"That's because there is no known way," Everett said with a sigh, rolling to his side and throwing the covers back. "Might as well get me dressed. She won't leave till she's had her say."

"Do you know why she's here, my lord?"

"Let's just say I have a guess."

A quarter of an hour later, Everett steeled himself and entered the dining room. He had known a confrontation with his mother was coming, sooner or later, but he was a bit surprised that it was sooner. He'd thought he at least had until he won Pippa over . . . but then, that was taking longer than he'd thought it would. With the *ton* now aware of the gentlemen following her around, to the point where invitations were being sent, he supposed it was only inevitable his mother had discovered what was going on.

Likely one of her friends had decided Lady Essex's attendance was necessary at their ball, to entice the gentlemen there, and had decided to brave his mother's ire. He could only imagine how *that* conversation must have gone.

Sitting straight as a fence post, his mother glared at him from across the dining room table. While there was a cup of tea in front of her, she did not appear to have asked for any food. Stopping by one of the footmen, Everett asked for coffee and a full breakfast, as well as toast and preserves for his mother. She had a weakness for preserves. Perhaps they would sweeten her mood.

From the way she continued to glare at him as he took his seat, it was likely a vain hope.

Rather than beat around the bush, Everett decided to take on the dragon straight on. There was no reason to play coy and prolong the inevitable.

"Well, Mother, what brings you to my house so early in the morning?"

The lines around her mouth tightened, her glare intensifying. The cold light of the morning gleamed against the grey that threaded through her perfectly coiffed hair. She was every inch a lady of the *ton*, but she did not represent the best of what Society had to offer. Even though she was his mother and he loved her, Everett had come to realize how manipulative and controlling she was.

"You are pursuing that . . . that trades girl again." She glared at him.

Everett's eyebrows rose and he pushed down the anger that filled his chest. "Do you mean the Dowager Countess of Essex?"

"Just because she was successful at title-hunting does not make her a lady," his mother said with a sneer. "The *ton* knows what she truly is."

"The *ton* does not seem to care." It was the wrong thing to say. Fire flashed in the duchess's eyes at the reminder that she'd been thwarted.

"You will cease your . . . interactions with that woman *immediately*," she hissed, leaning forward. "You are *ruining* your chances of a good marriage by being seen with her. You are making a mockery of our house and our good name, and a laughingstock of your father and I, being seen with such a low—"

"Stop. Right. There." Everett snapped out the words,

standing up to his full height as his own temper consumed him. His mother rocked back in her seat in shock, both at being interrupted and at his temerity. "No one cares about who her father was except you. Otherwise, you would not have had to threaten to withhold your own presence to ensure her lack of invitations—yes, I know about that. As for my chances at a good marriage, my *only* chance at marriage is with her. It is her or no one."

Gasping, obviously reeling at being stood up to, the duchess pressed her hand against her chest. "Everett . . . you cannot possibly . . . she will not . . . *I* will not stand for it! You need an heir! And a marriage with a lady from a good family—"

"There is nothing wrong with Lady Essex's family!" He interrupted her again, and he truly thought she might pass out from the shock of it. "Not the one she married into nor the one she was born into. If she will not have me, then cousin Albert will be my heir."

Her face so white she looked sickly, the duchess shook her head, her mouth opening and then closing. Seeing the footman bringing his breakfast in, Everett calmly sat down. But he should not have let his guard down so soon.

It only took long enough for him to cut off a bite of sausage for his mother to recover herself. Color was rushing back into her face as she worked herself into a fine fury, going from pale white to bright red in a matter of moments.

"I will not have it. Your father and I will *not* have it. We will cut you off entirely. You will have nothing, and you will have to *beg* for your allowance, you will have to marry whatever woman I choose . . ."

She ranted, Everett ate his breakfast. It took her several

minutes to realize he was unmoved by her speech. He needed every ounce of his willpower to pretend complete indifference. What he really wanted to do was shout at her, but he also just felt tired.

Tired of her manipulations, tired of her threats, tired of her thinking she could run every aspect of his life. He had tried for so long to be a dutiful son, but the moment he wanted to make a choice for himself that she did not agree with . . . this was how she reacted. As if she would somehow be affected by who he married.

Her snobbery disgusted him almost as much as her threats.

Pressing her lips together, she stood. Everett jumped up as well, his good manners too ingrained to do anything else.

"This isn't over," she said, her voice low and threatening, before she swept from the room in as dramatic an exit as she could manage.

Feeling exhausted for reasons that had nothing to do with his interrupted sleep, Everett slowly sat down again. He leaned against the back of his chair with a sigh. The Duke of Beaufort's house party could not come a moment too soon.

CHAPTER ELEVEN

"OH . . . *OH* . . . MARCUS!" THROWING HER
head back, Philippa gasped and shuddered against the
chaise.

Katherine had left them to their tea, thoughtfully
closing the door behind her, and after a few more minutes
of conversation, Marcus had affirmed his interest in
continuing their friendship. She had dressed for the occasion, in a gown with a wide, low neckline that was easily
pulled down in front so he could lavish attention on her
breasts before lifting her skirts and diving beneath them.

She was eager to have him there, remembering how
skillful he'd been in the carriage. Now, with more room
to work, the pleasure was even greater. His tongue danced
over her sensitive flesh, teasing her swollen pleasure bud,
and then his fingers slipped inside of her. The sensation of
being penetrated overwhelmed her, and her body clenched
around the thrusting digits, a small orgasm shuddering
through her almost immediately.

But Marcus did not stop, the way she thought he
might. If anything, the sounds of her pleasure spurred him
onwards, his tongue and fingers working to bring her to a

higher peak. She ground her pussy against his lips, fingers threaded through his hair, desperately seeking the pinnacle.

"Oh *yes!*"

His fingers curved inside of her, touching that most exquisitely sensitive spot, and Philippa exploded in white-hot ecstasy. Moaning, writhing, she completely lost herself to the rapture as Marcus suckled at her clit with long pulls that drew her through wave after wave of erotic bliss until she finally went limp.

Panting, she blinked up at him as he rose above her. He quickly undid his breeches.

Finally!

Although, she was not sure how much more pleasure her body could take . . .

His intentions were not what she'd thought, though. Rather than settling between her thighs, he took his hand, wet with the slick honey of her arousal, and wrapped it around his cock. Philippa blinked, uncertain of what to do, as his hand pumped once . . . twice . . . and then there was nothing *to* do. It had all happened so quickly and she was still discombobulated from her orgasm.

Jets of white seed sprayed over her breasts, hot spatters decorating her skin. It was very unexpected, but not entirely unpleasant. Watching Marcus in the throes of his own pleasure was stimulating in its own right, and she did not mind the mess on her chest—she was too fascinated. Clarence had never done anything like that.

Gingerly, she touched one of the dripping streaks with her fingertips. Her husband had never found his culmination anywhere but inside her. The fluid was rather slimy, even without her cream. Fascinating. Katherine would probably call it unhygienic, but Philippa did not mind.

When she returned her attention to Marcus, he was panting, watching her touch the stuff while he laced his breeches back up. Hand dipping into his jacket, he pulled out a handkerchief.

"Here, allow me," he said.

It took everything she had not to laugh as he decorously cleaned his seed off of her breasts. She was sure Katherine would be in fits when they talked later, if Philippa could even bring herself to speak of this. By the time Marcus left half an hour later, Philippa knew she would need to say something. She was very confused by the emptiness still hounding her . . . she felt satisfied, but somehow also like something was missing, and she did not understand what.

And she still did not know what to do about Hartington.

After the confrontation with his mother, Everett knew it was only a matter of time before his father joined the fray. To his surprise, rather than calling upon him directly, his father sent a note through his solicitor informing him that he would no longer be authorized to draw funds from the estate until he agreed to "behave more reasonably." Snorting, Everett threw the letter down on his blotter, unconcerned.

His parents had not been keeping as close a watch on him as they once had, and they clearly had no idea that he did not need their money. Likely there would be other forms of retribution headed his way once they realized not only that he was not falling into line, but that his bills were still being paid. That they intended to freeze him out until he came around to their way of thinking would actually give him more time before their next move.

If only he were able to make better use of it.

Each evening that passed was frustrating, even when he did manage to claim a dance with Philippa, but it also brought him closer to Beaufort's house party. Everett was beginning to feel as though he was passing time till then. The helplessness he felt to actually *do* something was the hardest part. Being bound by Society's rules at the balls, there was very little he *could* do.

Visiting her at-homes was just as fruitless.

His main consolation was that Conyngham seemed to be faring about as poorly. Philippa's presence at the larger balls and soirees meant even more competition for both of them, and the crowd of gentlemen around her drew even more of them. Thanks to Sunderland, he also knew that Conyngham had been successful visiting her outside of the at-homes once, but not again since then.

Everett had decided not to try. It felt too much like giving her the chance to reject him, and he did not want her to become too practiced at doing so. Better to show her he was a changed man . . . that he would happily wait for her this time, that he would not be put off by his competition, and that he truly did mean it when he said he loved her and wished to wed her.

Three nights before Beaufort's house party, Everett nearly fell over when she turned to him and asked him to walk her about the room in between the dances.

"Me?" he asked stupidly, wondering if he had suddenly stepped into a dream. For days, she had ignored him unless forced to acknowledge him, and her request was more than unexpected—it actually shocked him.

"Unless your feet are too weary from standing," she replied, a twinkle in her eye. "I'm sure one of these other fine gentlemen—"

"No, no," he interrupted her, grasping onto the opportunity to speak with her privately—at least as privately as they could possibly be. A promenade was much better than a dance for conversation. "I am very happy to escort you, my lady."

Holding out his arm, he felt a surge of happy triumph when she smiled up at him and placed her fingertips gently on his sleeve. There was a touch of wariness in her eyes, but there was more than that too. Something that she must want to say to him without an audience.

They moved away from the others, and Everett's heart was pounding in his chest with anticipation. Unfortunately, as he'd had no time to prepare, he had no idea what to say to her now that he had the chance. It turned out not to matter, as she had something to say to him—well, to ask him.

"Why are you doing this?" She turned her head slightly, tilting her chin to peer up at him from the corner of her eye.

"I thought you wanted to stretch your legs," he said, immediately confused. She *had* been the one to suggest the walkabout.

"Not this, *this*." She waved her fan between them. "Why are you still pursuing me? It's been days and you have made no headway, I have given you no sign of returning your supposed affections, and yet still you come to dance attendance on me with the others."

"I told you before. My reasons have not changed."

Turning her head away, she nibbled on her lower lip. "I have taken a lover."

The announcement was said softly, almost apologetically, but she said it all the same. Everett's chest seized, but on this topic, he was used to that by now. "Mr. Horn, yes?"

Utter shock ground her to a halt, and Lord Bardwell almost ran into her from behind before Everett managed to tug her out of the way.

"You know?" She gasped out the words.

"Conyngham told me after he and Sunderland ran into you leaving Horn's carriage." Everett managed to keep his voice even by sheer force of will, but he could not entirely hide his emotions. Especially not from Philippa. Clenching his jaw, he met her sapphire eyes so he could impress upon her the utter sincerity of his next words. "I told you. I love you. I understand you fell out of love with me, but that does not change my heart nor my determination to win yours back."

For the second time in her life, Philippa felt close to swooning. Perhaps it was no coincidence that both times were so closely linked to the man whose arm she was on, but the first time had been a terrible moment. This . . . this was . . . unexpected, certainly. Her feelings ricocheted around her chest, too quickly for her to really grasp.

How could he still want to *marry* her . . . how could he have continued pursuing her, all the while knowing . . . It did not make sense.

Not unless . . .

He loved her.

Panic gripped her.

Somehow, and she did not know how, she managed to keep her composure as Hartington silently returned her to their circle. Thankfully, he seemed to understand that she needed time to digest this new revelation, and he did not attempt to drum up conversation again. He just bowed over her hand, his fingers pressing against hers for one heart-stoppingly intimate moment, and then he pulled away.

No . . . not just pulled away. He left.

For the first time, he left the ball before she did.

And she felt his absence.

Beaufort's house party could not come soon enough. She needed to get away. Away from London. Away from everything and everyone. Especially all these men.

She needed to think.

Leaving Hathaway House, Everett did not know why he felt compelled to walk away, but he knew he needed some space. He could not stand another long evening of watching Philippa and all the gentlemen gathered around her. All of them vying to be her next—or perhaps an additional—lover.

There was a part of him that wondered how he could still want her, but then he remembered what it had been like to lose her before. How it had felt to know that she'd married another, that she'd never be *his*. He'd been granted a second chance at the life he had dreamed of. He would be foolish not to take it.

Yes, they had both changed. They had grown, matured. Philippa might be more cynical now, but her soft heart was still there. He saw it in the way she made sure to pay some attention to each gentleman who made up her circle, even those who were less attractive, less wealthy, and less interesting. He saw it in the way she arranged for her companion to be available to Sunderland, rather than insisting the woman remain by her side.

While she might claim she no longer wanted love and marriage, there was still romance in her soul.

Withdrawing from the field might be a great error or it might reap some reward if she missed his presence. If she did not . . . well, indifference was an answer all on its own. But so far she did not seem indifferent to him. Just undecided.

Hm.

Perhaps for the next two nights he would make himself scarce. Remind her of what life without each other's company was like . . . and then he would surprise her with his presence at Beaufort's.

"Where is he?" Philippa muttered under her breath, tapping her fan impatiently against her thigh.

The morning after the Hathaway ball, the flower arrangement from Hartington had arrived as it always did, but he had not appeared at the Dunbury's ball that evening. His absence had increased her anxiety to a shocking degree, making her temperamental all evening— to her dismay. She did not like that he could still affect her so.

But of course she was affected. Both Olivia and Katherine had become misty-eyed when she'd told them of his words. Olivia was sure it meant he truly loved her. Katherine was more skeptical, but still thought it showed him to be a higher quality man than the usual sort—one who would not let his pride rule him.

Leaving Philippa with the burning question of whether or not she wanted to give Hartington a second chance at her heart.

She had to admit, she was still attracted to him. He

did seem as though he had grown in their time apart, all in ways that she appreciated. But she had changed, too. Did he really know her? Or did he think that once he had gained her love that she would revert back to the same trusting, easily led, wide-eyed innocent that she'd been the first time they fell in love? Because Philippa did not think she could pretend to be that girl again, not even for someone she loved.

She was older, wiser, and stronger. She had her own income, her own social status, and her own place in the world. Going by the number of gentlemen thronging to her, she had her choice of lovers or suitors, depending on what she wanted. There was still a small part of her that worried over her own skills as a lover, but surely that could be rectified with practice.

That was something she was not sure she would ever receive with Mr. Horn. Olivia had gone searching for gossip, and it seemed that what Katherine had overheard was only a small part of his inclinations . . . he truly enjoyed giving a woman pleasure with his tongue, to the exclusion of all else. Philippa did not object to being on the receiving end of his attentions, but she also wanted to *do* something.

When it came to a man, she was beginning to realize she wanted a partnership. She did not know if such a thing would be possible with Hartington as a lover, much less a husband.

CHAPTER TWELVE

"THIS IS EXACTLY WHAT I NEEDED," PHILIPPA said to Katherine, falling back onto the bed of her guest room in Bellham Hall, the Duke of Beaufort's house. Katherine's room was right next door, smaller and less grand than Philippa's but just as comfortable and elegantly furnished. The rose and cream décor of both rooms was both beautiful and feminine, making Philippa feel like she was in a garden.

"For me as well," Katherine admitted, coming to sit on the foot of the bed and leaning against the post.

Philippa looked at her in surprise. "Really? I was feeling rather guilty, taking you away from Lord Sunderland's company."

"He is exactly why I am relieved to be out of the city for a few days," Katherine said with a wistful kind of sigh. "He is . . . very confusing."

Raising one eyebrow, Philippa smirked at her companion. "Is he? Or are you just confused by your emotions in regard to him?"

"I could ask the same of you," Katherine retorted, and Philippa made a face.

"I would much rather you did not."

Both of them were laughing when there came a knock at the door and they exchanged a confused look. It was the first afternoon, which meant there should be no scheduled events until dinner, and Philippa did not think anyone even knew of her presence. Well, anyone other than their host. She and Katherine had the thought at the same time, and they both jumped to their feet.

Katherine answered the door while Philippa attempted to brush the wrinkles out of her skirt. She had not yet taken the time to change from her traveling dress and she assumed she must look a fright.

Keeping the door mostly closed, Katherine turned to address her. "If it's convenient, the Duke of Beaufort would like you to join him for a drink in his study." She tilted her head at Philippa. "Half an hour?"

The question was whether or not Philippa could be presentable by then. Half an hour was tight but doable, and it would not keep the duke waiting for too long. She nodded, immediately moving toward the armoire where the servants had hung her gowns when they'd arrived.

Twenty-five minutes later, she was presentable in a dark blue gown that made her eyes shine brightly. Katherine twisted her hair up into a simple but elegant chignon. A strand of grey pearls that rested against the tops of her breasts completed the look, leaving Philippa feeling less like she had been traveling all day and more like she was a lady ready for anything.

A servant knocked on her door exactly half an hour from when Katherine had last answered it and escorted her to the duke's study. He was at his desk, but he stood as soon as she was announced. At home, he was just as handsome and stately as he had been when he was the guest, but here he appeared even more comfortable and secure than ever. Perhaps it was as simple as being in his own domain.

"Ah, my lady, thank you for indulging me," he said, hurrying around his desk to greet her again. "I hope my invitation did not interrupt your afternoon."

"Certainly not, your grace," she said with a smile, giving him a hand to kiss.

An odd light came into his eyes as he pressed his lips against her hand, making her wonder—as she had the entire time she was dressing—why he had invited her to such an intimate meeting.

He led her over to one of the chairs in front of his desk, but rather than retreating behind the large piece of furniture, he sat in the leather armchair directly next to the one he seated her in. Philippa pushed down her surprise, waiting for him to speak first, as she could not fathom what he might wish to speak with her about.

Unexpectedly, he fussed with his cravat, clearing his throat and looking more uncomfortable than she'd ever seen him before. "Lady Essex . . . I ah . . . I have a sort of proposal for you."

"A proposal?" She blinked, and then laughed. She still could not imagine what he might want from *her*. Surely he did not mean . . .

"Yes, a proposal," he said, more firmly than he had before. Philippa received the impression that he was gathering his confidence. "A marriage proposal."

Her lips parted in shock, her thoughts reeling, as those were the *last* words she'd ever expected to come out of his mouth.

The expression on his face was almost apologetic, and he leaned toward her, his words coming quickly and earnestly now that he had broached the topic. "I need an heir and for that, I need a wife. You are accomplished, intelligent, attractive, and I believe we would get on well."

"I do not have a dowry." Those were the first words out of her mouth, which was a measure of how flabbergasted she was. But during her time as a debutante, that had been why most of the gentlemen were interested in her. It had been the reason Clarence had proposed. Hartington . . . well, he had not been interested in her dowry. He had not needed it.

Of course, Beaufort did not either.

He chuckled. "I would expect to be the one settling an income on you, my dear, not the other way round in this case."

Philippa smiled, but it was a polite smile. A demure smile. One that covered her emotions as she searched for the words to gently turn him down. With Hartington it had been easier because she had been trying to drive him away; with Beaufort, she did not want to be crass or rude.

"You may have heard about my mistress, and it is true, I have a long-term relationship with her, and I do not intend to end it. However, once I have my heir, I would not interfere with any of your activities either," Beaufort said, completely diverting her thoughts. This was the second shock of the conversation. Beaufort was being audacious with his openness, but Philippa had to appreciate his honesty. He gave her a look. "I know Clarence did not hold the same view, but I am not so possessive or hypocritical."

"What if I could not provide an heir?" she asked, to

give herself more time to think. "I know Clarence and I were not married for long, but . . ." She had never shown any sign of pregnancy, despite how active he had been in the marital bed. At first she'd been sad, as she would have liked children, but at his death she'd thought perhaps it had been for the best.

Shocking her for a third time, Beaufort merely shrugged. "Helena and I have been together for over a decade now, and she has never been with child. The fault may be mine, I do not know. If that were the case, then after three years, you may consider yourself free to—discreetly—pursue lovers outside of our marriage. If a child were to come from such a union, I would acknowledge them and treat them as my own."

The offer was excessively generous. Philippa realized she was tempted. Partly because it would be familiar, safe . . . marriage to a man who did not love her but whom she did not love either. Marriage to a *duke*, no less. A little burble of excitement bubbled up inside of her, making her feel slightly ashamed when she realized where it came from: thinking about facing Hartington's mother as a social equal. Someone who did not need fear her, who could not be touched by her in any manner . . .

That was not a good enough reason to be married.

"What about Helena? Could I meet her?" Philippa was more than a little curious about the other woman. She wondered why Beaufort did not marry *her*, although the lack of children might be reason enough. The length of their relationship and his honesty about his unwillingness to give her up made it clear she was of great importance to him.

Beaufort shifted uncomfortably in his chair. "Now?"

"She's here?" Philippa blurted the question out. She'd meant if she considered his suit, but if the woman was actually here at the manor . . . Her curiosity welled higher.

To her amusement, Beaufort actually blushed, looking more like a schoolboy than a grown duke. "Yes, well . . . I do not like to be far from her."

"I would very much like to meet her then," Philippa said. She had never met any of Clarence's mistresses. "I do not know if I can seriously consider your proposal. I had made up my mind not to marry again but . . . if I am to consider it, I would need to meet her. I promise I will not be unkind I just . . . I need to."

Philippa did not know if she could marry a man who loved another. She also wanted to know why Beaufort would not marry the woman he loved. Perhaps meeting this Helena would help clarify matters.

"She will not be at dinner tonight." Beaufort sighed, looking resigned to the fact and slightly resentful. "Perhaps you could join us after dinner?"

"That would be acceptable."

Leaving a bemused Beaufort to his thoughts, Philippa left to return to Katherine, already wondering at this turn of events. Two marriage proposals now, when all she had wanted was a lover. The first from an eventual duke, the second from a current one.

Certainly, marriage to Beaufort would be easier, in many respects. It would change her life in ways even marriage to Clarence had not. But she also knew she would certainly lose Hartington forever if she did so. Two weeks ago, she might have considered that a good reason to immediately accept . . . now she was not so sure.

* * *

Everett had not arrived at Beaufort's house party alone.

Once he'd realized what was in the wind, Roger had insisted on accompanying him, and he'd let Miss Parrish's location drop to Sunderland, who had then begged to tag along. The man was smitten, and Everett too sympathetic to deny him. The woman was leading him on a merry chase. Fortunately, a quick note to Beaufort had confirmed that his friends would be welcome.

They were all shown to three rooms in the same hall, which Everett assumed housed all the unattached gentlemen who were attending the party. Hopefully he'd be able to find out where the unattached *ladies* were sleeping. Not that he planned on sneaking into Philippa's room tonight, but it never hurt to be prepared.

They were among the first to arrive in the parlor before dinner. As guests began to fill the room, Everett was relieved to see they were mostly older couples, although a few did have their sons and daughters with them. Of course, the mothers immediately brought their daughters over to be introduced to Everett and his companions.

The three bowed over their hands, complimented their dresses, and did their best not to engage too fully with any one young lady. Roger, in particular, looked like he was regretting insisting on accompanying Everett. Unlike Sunderland, he had no other motive for being there.

When Pippa finally entered the room, arm in arm with her companion, it was like all the air was sucked out of his lungs by the sheer magnificence of her presence. The bright blue of her dress matched her eyes exactly, the sapphires around her neck enhancing the pale cream of her skin. There was a great deal of skin showing, and Everett's cock twitched as he imagined dropping kisses over every exposed inch.

She turned her head, their eyes caught across the room, and she came to an abrupt halt. Emotions flashed across her face, too quick to catch, but the general impression Everett received was not a welcoming one. She was not happy to see him there.

Perhaps he had miscalculated, leaving her alone the past few nights even though he'd continued sending flowers. Coming in behind her, the Marquess and Marchioness of Hertford caught sight of him as well. The marquess gave him a stern glare while the marchioness stared suspiciously. Whatever goodwill he had built up with her, it was not enough that she was pleased to see him.

"She does not seem happy to see you," Roger murmured, confirming Everett's impression.

Pippa tore her gaze away, giving him the freedom to turn and glare at his friend. "She was not expecting to see me," he corrected, deciding to remain hopeful. "I am sure she will be more welcoming once she gets over the shock."

"Katherine does not seem pleased to see me either," Sunderland said with a sigh. He was gazing longingly across the room at the woman who was steadfastly avoiding meeting his eyes. Seeing Sunderland so love-sick would have been amusing, if Everett did not feel the exact same way. The two of them together made for a depressing pair.

"You two are both hopeless," Roger muttered.

"What would you know about it?" Sunderland asked, jabbing a finger at him. "You have never been in love." His statement made both Everett and Roger stare at him.

Realizing what he'd said, Sunderland jerked his gaze away from them, his jaw muscle clenching.

There was no time to question each other further, however. Beaufort entered the room just before the dinner bell rang and they were paired off to escort a lady into dinner. Unfortunately, Beaufort himself took Pippa's arm, leaving Everett to offer his to two elderly ladies rather than brave one of the younger ones. Sunderland managed to secure a place beside Miss Parrish, who did not appear happy about it, and poor Roger was left to escort a giggling young miss.

For all of Everett's hopes of using the house party to secure some time alone with Pippa, it was not as easy as he'd supposed. They were too far away during dinner to converse, even if she had looked in his direction, and he was forced to focus on those around him. At the end of dinner, Beaufort stood and welcomed everyone before suggesting they were all likely tired from traveling during the day and that they retire early so they could be refreshed for tomorrow.

To Everett's frustration, everyone thought this was a splendid idea.

Not that everyone retired immediately. Several of the older gentlemen ambled off to the library for cigars and brandy, a group of ladies went in search of the music room, and the younger set were eager to play charades in the parlor. Everett wanted to be wherever Pippa was, but she was nowhere to be found, and after an hour of searching he and Sunderland were forced to admit defeat. Roger had refused to help them and had gone back to his own room rather than be coerced into the game of charades.

Likely she'd retired for the night rather than face him.

Resigned, Everett slunk back to his own room. Tomorrow she would not be able to avoid him so easily, and she would have all night to adjust her expectations of the party to include his presence.

CHAPTER THIRTEEN

AFTER THE SHOCK OF SEEING HARTINGTON at dinner, Philippa almost sent Beaufort a note to say she was too tired for their meeting that evening, but Olivia and Katherine both insisted she still go. She suspected their interest was somewhat prurient, but she allowed herself to be convinced.

She still wanted to meet Beaufort's mistress. Still was tempted by Beaufort's proposal.

Still tempted by Hartington's proposal as well, but his felt like a riskier proposition. With Beaufort, well she already knew what that kind of marriage would be like. There would be no surprises, no risks . . . and no love. Genuine affection they already had, though, and she could look for love again in a few years if she desired it. Love with someone who had not already betrayed her.

But only if she truly did not want to give Hartington another chance. Which she was very torn on.

A servant came to fetch her and led her back to Beaufort's bedroom. She was slightly surprised at first, and then realized it was likely the one place where he could guarantee they would not be interrupted. He did have a house full of guests after all.

She had not changed out of her gown from dinner yet and felt a bit overdressed when she entered the room to find Beaufort inside, no longer wearing his coat. There was a woman, older than Philippa but younger than Beaufort, standing by his side, nervously pressing her hands together in front of her. The gown she was wearing was low cut, and the dark red color against her pale skin and dark hair was a beautifully dramatic contrast.

"My lady," Beaufort said, stepping forward, almost as if to shield his mistress in case Philippa reacted badly. "This is Helena Martin. Helena, this is the Dowager Countess of Essex."

Helena curtsied and Philippa stepped forward, holding out her hands, which Helena automatically took.

"Please, call me Philippa." Helena's dark eyes widened in surprise, but she nodded shyly. It felt very odd to realize she intimidated the older woman. Philippa smiled at her, hoping to set her further at ease. "Thank you for agreeing to meet me."

The gratitude and relief on Beaufort's face was easy to see, as was the love in his eyes when he looked at Helena. A sense of yearning rose up inside of Philippa, but she pushed it away. Her first love story had not ended well—theirs might not either. Beaufort needed an heir, for which he needed a wife. His honesty about the situation meant he would hopefully be able to find an understanding one, but there were no guarantees.

"I . . ." Helena started to speak and then stopped. Philippa smiled encouragingly at her, but Helena still looked to Beaufort before continuing in a soft voice. "I am not sure why you wished to meet me, my . . . um, Philippa."

Releasing Helena's hands, Philippa continued to smile at her as she sat down in a chair near the bed. Helena settled onto the bed itself, her hands resting in her lap, while Beaufort leaned against the bedpost at the foot of the bed.

"Has the duke told you about my late husband?" Philippa asked. Helena nodded and Beaufort stirred.

"Not very much," Helena said. "Just that you were married before to a friend of his."

Philippa nodded. The duke was discreet. That he had not shared her personal business, even with the person closest to him, was a good sign. It made her feel as though she could trust him.

"Clarence had several mistresses," Philippa said bluntly. "As a new bride, it made me feel quite uncertain about myself, despite his attempts to reassure me. While I appreciate, ah, Curtis's honesty, I do not want a marriage such as that again. To be truthful, I'm not sure I wish to be married again at all." Somehow it was easier to say that here, now, perhaps because they were already being so open with each other. The duke nodded, as if unsurprised, and Philippa relaxed slightly. "But if I am to be married again, I do not want things to be hidden from me."

A tightness eased in her chest as she realized that was also why she was so wary of Hartington's offer, and why the duke's was so tempting. She still worried over the hidden dangers of being wed to Hartington, whereas the duke had been completely honest and open with her from the moment he made his proposal. And, unlike Hartington, he came without any previous hurts committed against her.

"If you do not want anything hidden away . . . would you wish to join us?" Helena asked, tilting her head to the side.

"Join you?" Philippa was confused. The only possible interpretation she could think of to Helena's statement was . . . no. She must have that wrong.

Helena's gaze sharpened, her attention focusing on Philippa. Interestingly, the duke seemed content to let Helena take the lead here, perhaps seeing this as a negotiation between the woman in his life and a woman who might be soon in his life.

"Did Curtis tell you anything about me?" she asked, and Philippa shook her head. "He found me in a brothel when I was eighteen. He chose me out of a line of light-skirts, and he was my first client. Afterwards, he paid the madam my debt and took me with him. But before him, the other women there showed me many things, including how to pleasure another woman. Sometimes the men desired more than one lady in bed with him, you see."

Oh my. Philippa's first thought *had* been correct. She could not deny that her curiosity was roused now. To be a *part* of things in a way Clarence had never allowed her to be? That was something she had never anticipated. She also had no doubt that there were many things *she* could learn from Helena.

"How . . . how would that work?"

Helena's face lit up and she stood, a few quick steps bringing her directly in front of Philippa.

"Let me show you," she murmured, cupping Philippa's

cheeks to tilt her head back and slowly lowering her lips to Philippa's.

Shocked, intrigued, Philippa did not move away, although Helena gave her time to. Her eyes closed as she was kissed by another woman for the first time.

Helena's lips were soft. She tasted like mint. The kiss was gentle and coaxing, seductive rather than forceful. Philippa's lips parted with Helena's, and she shivered when Helena's tongue slipped into her mouth. The other woman was a very good kisser, although there was an ineffable difference between kissing her and kissing a man. Philippa could not describe it, only that she was sure that if Helena and ten men all kissed her while she was blindfolded, she would know which kiss came from Helena.

The hands cupping her face slid down to her shoulders and then to her arms, and Philippa allowed Helena to draw her up out of the chair so they could kiss more fully. Helena was several inches shorter than Philippa and, for the first time, Philippa was the one with her head tilted down to kiss. It was both an odd and interesting experience.

Breasts pressed against her, just under her own. Small, gentle hands explored her sides. Philippa's nipples hardened, her pussy becoming soft and slick. It did not matter that Helena was a woman—what she was doing felt very, very good.

"Oh my . . ." Philippa said when Helena pulled her lips away and began kissing down Philippa's neck. Her eyes opened and she met the duke's gaze. He was watching them with rapt arousal, although he had not moved from his post by the bed. Knowing he was watching excited

Philippa even more for some reason. The laces of her dress gave as Helena pulled on them, and she gasped.

"Tell me if you want to stop," Helena whispered, tugging the front of Philippa's dress down to reveal her breasts. Small, soft kisses made their way across her bosom, and Philippa's breath came in faster and faster pants. She definitely did not want to stop.

The forbidden nature of what they were doing made it all the more exciting. A woman was touching her and a man—a duke—was watching. Would he even join them? This was the kind of erotic adventure she had not even suspected was possible, but now that it was being offered, she could not possibly turn it down. She also had the excuse of wanting to know everything about what being married to the Duke of Beaufort would be like.

If this was part of it, then she should know.

She moaned as Helena's lips went lower, sucking one pert nipple into her mouth. Helena's cheeks were softer than a man's against Philippa's breasts, her suction gentler but no less urgent.

Feeling very bold, Philippa let her own fingers travel over Helena's body, exploring Helena's neck and shoulders. The duke stood silently watching, shrugging off his waistcoat and beginning to work on his shirt sleeves. Excitement curdled low in Philippa's belly as she realized the next stage of this was about to start.

"Strip her, love." The order was given in a low, growling voice, and it took Philippa a moment to realize he was speaking to Helena.

The other woman eagerly began to undress Philippa, tugging the gown fully off of her before moving to undo her corset. The duke was slowly undressing himself, revealing a fine figure of a man. Older, yes, with grey sprinkled through the hair on his chest and bit of roundness over his stomach, but still fit and appealing to look upon. His cock jutted out of a nest of dark curls and he wrapped his hand around it, slowly pumping while he watched Helena undress Philippa.

"Now, Philippa, strip Helena."

Being ordered about was not something Philippa would have expected to arouse her, but it did. Perhaps because she did not have to think of what to do next, the duke had told her exactly what he wanted. This was all entirely new to her, so a bit of direction helped her feel more confident.

He continued to fist his manhood as Philippa undressed Helena, revealing a body slightly rounder than her own. The most shocking moment was when she removed Helena's drawers to reveal a woman's mound entirely lacking in covering. The skin above Helena's pussy was completely shorn, making it possible to see all the soft, dark, pink folds between her legs.

Helena giggled when Philippa gasped. "Curtis prefers me bare."

"Do you like it?" Philippa asked, unable to tear her gaze away. She had seen other women's bodies before, but never like this.

"I do." Helena reached out and took Philippa's hand, pressing it to her mound and curving Philippa's fingers over the area. Philippa's fingertips touched the slick wetness of Helena's arousal, and she nearly gasped again at the unfamiliar and rather exciting discovery. Helena let out a little moan. "I'm so sensitive this way. I can feel *everything*."

Still holding Philippa's hand in place, Helena rocked

her hips, rubbing the front of her pussy against Philippa's fingertips. The warm folds glided over Philippa's fingers. She stared down at where her hand was thrust between Helena's thighs, watching every small movement with utter fascination.

"Kiss again." The duke had moved up behind Philippa, and she felt the heat of his body from behind mere moments before his flesh touched hers. Helena's hand wrapped around the back of Philippa's neck, drawing her down for another kiss, while her other hand still moved Philippa's fingers between her thighs.

The duke's cock nestled between Philippa's buttocks, hot and hard, as he pressed her in between him and his mistress. The abundance of flesh against hers, rubbing and stimulating her on front and back, was nearly overwhelming. Lips pressed against the back of her neck. The duke kissed her over her shoulders, while his hands settled on her hips and then moved upwards.

Philippa wrapped her other arm around Helena for balance, clinging to the other woman while still rubbing her fingers through her pussy. The duke's hands touched first Helena's breasts and then Philippa's, moving back and forth between the two of them.

Gasping against Helena's mouth, Philippa wriggled as the duke pinched her nipples and rolled them between his fingers. Helena's kiss was becoming more passionate, more needy, as the duke explored both of their bodies. She pressed Philippa's hand further between her thighs, rubbing herself against Philippa's palm in wanton abandon.

A low growl rumbled through the duke's chest where it was pressed against Philippa's back, and then he pulled away.

"On the bed, ladies," he ordered, his voice gruff with need. "Philippa, on your back against the pillows and spread your legs. Helena, you're going to pleasure her."

The crass order was all the more exciting for its boldness, and Philippa hastened to do as she was told. Leaning against the pillows piled on the headboard, she felt almost like a kind of sacrifice, spread out on an altar. Helena climbed onto the bed after her, moving between Philippa's spread thighs and lowering her mouth to Philippa's pussy.

"Oh yes . . ." Philippa moaned as Helena's tongue slid between her swollen folds. The other woman was just as talented as Marcus, teasing and sucking Philippa's sensitive parts.

The duke watched for a few moments as his mistress used her tongue on Philippa, and then he climbed onto the bed as well, settling himself on his knees behind Helena. It was a position Clarence had sometimes enjoyed as well, mounting Philippa like a stallion did a mare. She had never been able to watch it from this angle though.

Never been able to see Clarence's face when he thrust inside of her, the way she could see the duke's as he thrust inside of his mistress. Helena cried out as she was penetrated, the tiny vibrations humming against Philippa's pussy. The duke began to ride her, hands gripping her hips, grunting as he worked himself in and out of her body.

She passed that on to Philippa, her fingers sliding into Philippa's needy channel, tongue licking frantically, as though she could send the pleasure she was receiving into Philippa. Crying out with passion, Philippa arched against Helena's mouth and buried her fingers in the other woman's hair. It was like Helena knew how best to touch her, how to please her . . . which very might well be the case.

Their combined lust spilled over. The sound of flesh slapping against flesh and pleasured moans filled the air. It was sinfully decadent.

Philippa was the first to climax, sobbing out her ecstasy as Helena's fingers and tongue sent her soaring. She could feel the duke's eyes on her, watching as she writhed and twisted in glorious fervor until she was spent.

Then he pulled Helena away, flipping her onto her back and pounding between her thighs with a frenzied lust that he'd clearly been holding back until now. Philippa watched with exhausted interest as the two reached their pinnacle together, bodies fused with an intimacy that made her chest ache with envy. She was there, but she might as well have not been.

They had included her, but she was a guest, and in this moment, she felt it. She did not feel jealousy or anger, she only wished that she could be with someone who looked at her the way the duke and Helena looked at each other.

Now, after having shared physical pleasure with them, she could see what made the difference, knew what had been lacking in her assignations with Marcus.

Love.

Emotion that would transcend the physical experience.

It was there, between the duke and Helena. It was what Philippa wanted. But she knew now, no matter how pleasurable this had been, she would not find it with them. Still, she did not protest when a tired Helena cuddled her close, including her in their postcoital glow. She craved the closeness, even if it was borrowed.

For now, this would do.

Tomorrow . . . well, tomorrow she might have to seriously consider Hartington's suit. If love was what was missing, what she truly desired, then perhaps she should give him another chance. The thought was terrifying, but then, love often was.

CHAPTER FOURTEEN

FIRST TO ARRIVE AT THE BREAKFAST TABLE, Everett inwardly vowed not to quit his seat until Philippa appeared. There was always the chance she might send for her breakfast and eat it in her rooms, but the Philippa he knew had always preferred to sit at the table. She'd once confided in him that it felt rude to seclude herself away for a meal. If she had not changed too much, then she would come to breakfast.

Sunderland joined him not long after, grumbling under his breath about the early hour, but he seemed as determined as Everett to wait the ladies out. Last night, once dinner had adjourned, Miss Parrish had vanished and he'd had as little luck hunting her down as Everett had had with Pippa.

As guest after guest arrived and then left, Everett began to tense and Sunderland appeared increasingly morose.

The mealtime was nearly over when Philippa finally appeared in the dining room, wearing a green morning gown with blue flowers decorating the fabric. Strands of her hair framed her face, giving her a softer look than usual. She came to a halt when she saw him, and he almost expected her to turn and flee, but instead a thoughtful expression came over her face. Miss Parrish was with her, but Everett only had eyes for Pippa.

He and Sunderland both jumped to their feet with much more alacrity than they had for any of the other ladies coming to breakfast. Exchanging quick glances, they moved to divide and conquer, Everett escorting Pippa to sit next to him at the table and Sunderland escorting Miss Parrish to the other side. It was only the barest semblance of privacy, but it would do. To Everett's relief, the ladies allowed it, although Pippa's expression was still inscrutable and she was quiet other than returning his "good morning." He could not decide if that was better or worse than the scolding Sunderland was receiving from Miss Parrish for not revealing that he would be coming to the house party.

She had told him of the plans to attend, apparently, and did not appreciate the "surprise."

Likely dinner had not given her the opportunity to upbraid him, as there had been an audience, but she was taking full advantage of the empty breakfast table now. Which was exactly what Sunderland and Everett had planned to do, although not exactly in this manner.

Everett gave Pippa a wary look. "Are you going to rebuke me as well?"

"I'm still deciding," she said, smiling up at the footman who brought her plate before returning her attention to Everett. "Did you know we were going to be here?"

"Yes." Honesty seemed the best—the *only*—way forward if he was to have a chance at winning Pippa over. "I was hoping to secure some time with you away from London and the other gentlemen."

A small smile curved her lips. "Away from the competition?"

"Exactly."

Looking down to butter her toast, the little smile widened. "The duke asked me to marry him last night."

Everett opened his mouth. Closed it. Shock reverberated through him. Now that was a wrinkle he had not anticipated.

"I do not believe I'm going to accept, although the offer was tempting," Pippa said calmly, as if she had not just upended his world only to set it to rights again. His breath whooshed out of him in a sigh of relief. The Duke of Beaufort had a lot to offer a bride, much more than Everett after his own parents had cut off his funds, even if he did have his own income.

"Why not?" he asked after a long moment, his voice only slightly strangled.

"He is in love with his mistress," Pippa said. "Seeing them together confirmed to me that if I *am* to marry again, I would like my husband to be in love with me, not another woman."

Picking up her toast to take a delicate bite, she looked at him expectantly, but Everett was still caught on part of her previous statement. "You *saw them* together?"

The duke had proposed marriage and then introduced Pippa to his mistress? The very boldness of such a move was both appalling and inspiring.

"I insisted on meeting her. We had a . . . very interesting night together." The little smile was much broader now, secretive, and Everett's imagination went wild. Jealousy, envy, lust, desire all surged inside of him, and he pushed back the emotions, struggling to control his reactions.

"Did you?" he asked, his voice rough. He clenched his fists on his lap and then relaxed them, opening and closing his fingers several times as he wrestled with himself. "Did you do so in order to test me?"

Her expression shifted, becoming almost scornful. "No, my lord. I spent the night with them for *me*. I am *telling* you about it in order to test you."

Pressing his lips together, Everett made himself sit quietly and watch Pippa finish her breakfast. Sunderland and Miss Parrish were conversing in low murmurs, the same way he and Pippa had been, so he could only catch a word or two, but they seemed to have reconciled.

Everett did not know what *he* was going to do. He wanted to ask that Pippa give him an answer now, about his own proposal, but he did not think he would get the answer he wished. Still, did he want to continue chasing after her like a lovesick pup while she had her merry way with whoever she wished? No. It was not just his pride speaking either.

It hurt, hearing what she was doing.

When she had finished her meal, she set down her tea and looked at him, tilting her head in question, waiting for him to say something.

"I would prefer not to hear about your assignations with others," he said, his voice clipped. "Please."

Pippa's eyebrows rose in surprise. "But you are not going to try to stop me from having them?"

"As you said, you owe me no loyalty." It galled him to admit that, but it was true. "I am the one trying to win you over, not the other way round. But I do not want to hear about it anymore." He paused for only a moment, his voice pitching even lower before he made his vulnerable confession. "It hurts to hear of it."

Her eyes softened, turning apologetic, and Everett knew she would agree even before she nodded.

"Would you like to escort me for a walk?" she asked.

"A walk?" he repeated stupidly, unsure if he'd heard her correctly. The jump in conversation was so abrupt, the request so unexpected, he almost thought he had imagined it.

"Yes, I hear the gardens here are quite lovely," she said, rising to her feet. On pure instinct, Everett rose with her. Her sapphire eyes were trained on his, full of hidden meaning. "Rather private as well."

This was his chance, he suddenly realized. She was giving him *a chance.*

"I think a walk sounds perfect," he said, offering his arm.

When Pippa took it and smiled up at him, his heart fairly sang.

Walking on Hartington's arm into the garden, Philippa's heart was pounding just like it had the first time he'd escorted her for a walk.

There were many differences between the first time and now, though.

Then, she had been flattered, breathless, and already completely enamored of the young lord. Stunned that he would even wish to speak with her. Hopeful, in the way only a young woman who had never been hurt could be. Now she was wary, anxious, and wondering if she had gone mad even considering giving him the opportunity to win her affections again.

"Do you still enjoy gardening?" he asked as they strolled down the path, his attention already on the flowers around them.

"I do," she said. "When I can find the time for it." During the very brief period she had been Clarence's wife, she had been thrilled at the opportunity to arrange his gardens the way she wanted. That duty now fell to the new countess, but it did not stop Philippa from getting her hands dirty when she wanted to.

To her surprise, conversation began to flow easily between them, almost as if no time had passed at all. She told him about her time on Clarence's estate—omitting the marital details of course—and he told her about how he'd gone into business, into *trade* of all things.

"My parents do not know, of course," he admitted. "My mother would likely have vapors for days."

Philippa could only imagine. Shaking her head, she could not keep the smile from her face.

This was a side to him that she had not known before—that he had not *had* before. Proud because of an accomplishment rather than the social status he had been born to, willing to work for what he wanted instead of demanding it be given to him, and confident. Perhaps not confident enough to tell his parents what he was doing, but that he was willing to defy them now said a great deal.

Coming to a halt amid the rose bushes, the sweet scent wreathing around them, Philippa looked up at him. "Kiss me."

Surprise widened his eyes, but she did not have to ask twice. Before she could second-guess herself, his lips were on hers, his mouth devouring her and taking her breath away.

He kissed her like he was drowning and she was the air he needed to breathe.

He kissed her like a man who was desperate to taste her, to hold her.

He kissed her like a man who wanted to claim her.

Philippa had *never* been kissed like this. Not by Helena or Marcus. Not by her husband. Not even by *him* before . . .

She kissed him back just as desperately, every part of her body yearning to press against him, to feel him, to be touched by him.

Only the voices suddenly audible in the air stopped them, bringing them back to their senses, and they broke apart, staring at each other wildly. She could still taste him on her swollen lips; her body was still tingling everywhere he had touched her.

"Everett . . ." She whispered his name, saying it for the first time since he'd broken her heart.

"Come with me, to my room," he whispered, his arms tightening around her.

She wanted to. Temptation beckoned, her body urging her to give in, but something held her back. Shaking her head, she stepped back, gently pressing her palms against his chest, and he released her.

"I need to think."

He dropped his hand. The pure longing on his face made her heart clench. "Whatever you need, Pippa."

His immediate acquiescence almost made her give in, but she really did need to think. Not just about how she felt about him, but what she wanted from him. She was beginning to truly believe he meant to marry her, but did she want to marry again? Was she ready to? Would it be fair to him to begin something she could not finish the way he hoped?

They walked back to the house, not touching, talking about small, inconsequential things. The weather. The flowers. His new horse. Philippa did not dare touch him again—she did not think she would be able to resist going with him if she did.

Instead, once they reached the house, she gave him one last look before walking away. She drifted down the hallway, feeling as though she were in a dream. A happy one.

Her lips lifted in a smile she could not quite push away.

Opening the door to her room, she blinked in surprise when she saw Katherine and Olivia waiting there for her, since she was expecting neither of them. Even more concerning, Katherine was pacing the room, her face red with fury, while Olivia was sitting in the window seat, face drawn and lips pressed tightly together.

"What is it?" Philippa asked, closing the door behind her. "What has Sunderland done?" It had to be Sunderland, because Katherine was clearly about to bubble over like a kettle.

"He told me the truth." Katherine spat out the words as Philippa made her way over to the window seat so she could settle beside Olivia. Both of them were looking at Philippa in a manner that made her skin crawl. Anger emanated off of them, but also sorrow, regret, and . . . pity? Katherine took a deep breath. "Hartington, Conyngham, they have a bet."

"A bet?" Philippa did not understand what that had to do with Katherine and Sunderland.

Anger faded further from Katherine's expression as she knelt down in front of Philippa, reaching out to take one of her hands. Olivia crowded in from the side, and a sick feeling began to creep through Philippa's stomach, a sour taste filling her mouth.

"They bet on you," Katherine said gently, squeezing Philippa's fingers. Olivia's arm wrapped around Philippa's shoulders in support, but she sat frozen, unable to speak much less move. "They bet to see who could seduce you first."

As Katherine explained, cold crept through Philippa, smoothing over the bubbling emotions and leaving nothing but ice in its wake.

After leaving Pippa at the house, Everett returned to the garden, ambling through and picking out various flowers. They were not in London, but he still wanted her to have her daily bouquet. It would be a bit smaller than usual, but handpicked flowers from a duke's garden were nothing to scoff at.

Eventually he made his way back inside, the flowers clutched in his hand. The ladies would likely be gathering for tea soon, which would be a perfect time to present the bouquet to her. Or perhaps he should do it less publicly, so as not to step on Beaufort's toes. While he wanted to stake his claim, Beaufort *was* his host. And from what Pippa had said, Everett did not need to worry she would accept Beaufort's suit.

Humming under his breath, he made his way back to his room, only stopping to ask a servant to have a vase and water sent there. He would have to hunt down some ribbon as well and find an appropriate moment to give Pippa the flowers.

Perhaps he could have a footman deliver them, to make it reminiscent of how he usually sent them.

But when he entered his hall, Sunderland was pacing in front of his door. When Everett turned the corner, Sunderland practically ran over to Roger's door and banged on it before turning to hiss at Everett. "Where have you *been?* I have been waiting for you for *ages!*"

"What's wrong?" Everett asked, frowning. He had never seen Sunderland so out of sorts.

The dour expression on Roger's face as he emerged from his own room did not bode well. He shot an almost pitying look at Everett.

"Inside," Sunderland ordered, shoving Everett into his own room and following him in. Roger came in last, shutting the door behind them.

"What happened?" Everett demanded to know again. The way his friends were acting had him pushing back panic. A million possibilities were flitting through his mind.

"She knows," Sunderland proclaimed in dire tones.

"Who knows what?"

"Lady Essex." The anguished apology on Sunderland's face made Everett's mouth go dry. "Katherine . . . she . . . . We were talking and she is very insistent on honesty and she talks very *quickly* sometimes, and it just slipped out and one thing led to another . . ."

"He told her about the bet," Roger said quietly from behind Everett.

Everett whirled around, dropping the flowers he'd been holding to the floor, only one thought in his mind. He had to get to Pippa. He had to *explain*. Sunderland did not know everything, he did not know how Everett felt about Pippa, he would not have known to tell Miss Parrish—

But Roger was still in front of the door.

"Get out of my way." Everett ground out the words.

"Think, man," Roger said urgently, not moving an inch. "Do you really want to do this? There is no way this can possibly end well."

"I have to try. I love her."

"Then why the hell did you make the bet about her in the first place?" Roger shouted the question, his face going red with anger. "Why not call it off? How can you claim to love her and still have made a bet about seducing her? Who *does* that?"

"You love her?" Sunderland asked, completely dumbfounded. "He *loves* her? I just . . . I just thought I had ruined the bet . . . you *love* her?"

That was the moment Everett realized that everything had truly gone tits up.

But it did not matter. He had to try to find Pippa. Try to explain the inexplicable. There was nothing else he could do.

"I do," he said, turning to Sunderland, no longer caring what his friends thought. No longer caring if they teased him or thought less of him. No longer caring if they saw him chase after Pippa and fail. "I have always loved her, despite my propensity for being a nodcock about it. Now, when did this happen? How long ago?"

"Hours," Sunderland replied, looking even more agonized than before, but still confused. "It has been more than two hours."

Everett closed his eyes as the enormity of the situation washed over him, but still he turned around to face Roger. Meeting his friend's gaze, he glared. "Move aside. Please."

Roger moved, resignation in every line of his body. He thought Everett was setting himself up for heartbreak again. That Pippa would reject him and never let him back into her heart now.

Rushing through the halls, he accosted several footmen before finding a maid who was able to tell him where the Dowager Countess of Essex's room was.

"But she's already gone," the maid said, as he started to race down the hall.

"Gone?" Everett whirled back around.

"Left in a hurry," the maid said, nodding her head, eyes alight with curiosity. "Not half an hour ago, with the Marquess and Marchioness of Hertford. Some kind of emergency back in London. Didn't even wait for their things to be packed, we're to be sending them on after them."

The frantic energy that had been buoying him up vanished, and Everett felt like dropping to the ground like he was a puppet whose strings had just been cut. Closing his eyes, he took several deep breaths, his mind racing.

What to do now?

CHAPTER FIFTEEN

RETURNING TO THE LONDON HOUSE BROUGHT Philippa no comfort.

Everett might not be there, but it did not matter. The anger, the frustration, the *hurt*, remained. All of which made her even more angry.

"I believed him," she muttered under her breath, pacing back and forth. "I believed him *again*."

While all along, he had merely been trying to win a bet. Not her trust. Not her heart. But he had broken both quite easily.

"It is not your fault," Katherine said, coming over and putting her arm around Philippa's shoulders. "Having faith in people is a good quality to have, even if it does not feel like it right now."

It certainly did not. Philippa leaned her head into Katherine's shoulder, seeking comfort from her friend. Her heart still felt sick. It was even worse than the first time because she was so very angry at *herself*. She should have known better.

"What are you going to do?" Katherine asked, after a long moment. "Shall we retreat from London?"

Retreat.

The way she had done the last time. She had fled, leaving Society and London to Everett. No, not Everett. Hartington, once again. Or *him*.

"No," she said slowly. "No, I will not retreat."

In fact, she was going to do something else entirely.

Her stomach churned as she walked up the stairs to Conyngham's house on Jermyn Street.

Respectable ladies did not visit this street. They certainly did not visit this street at this hour of the night, with a hooded cloak concealing their identity.

Hm. When she thought about it, perhaps if any other ladies of the *ton* ever did visit Jermyn Street, this was exactly how they dressed for the occasion. None of them would want anyone to know. If someone did recognize her, her reputation would be sullied and she would no longer be so welcome within Society. Olivia would have a conniption when she found out about this particular excursion, but Katherine had been just as incensed as Philippa, particularly over the delay in Sunderland telling her about the bet, and she had been feeling rather unreasonable as well.

Would she regret this tomorrow?

No. Philippa did not think so. Conyngham could just be another stop on her adventures. That had been her initial plan, which Everett had almost derailed with his . . . his kisses and his false promises and his silver tongue.

There was nothing she could do that would hurt him the way he'd hurt her—again—but she could ensure he lost his miserable little bet. If she found some pleasure in the activity, then all the better. Considering Conyngham's reputation, she was somewhat hopeful.

Before she could lose her nerve or second guess herself, she rapped on the door. It sounded uncommonly loud, making her wince, as she almost expected people to come running from the street to see who was making the ruckus. But no one came. After a long moment, during which her resolve began to waver, the door opened and she looked up to see Conyngham's handsome face. His cravat was untied but he was still dressed for the evening, likely having just returned home from whatever frolics he'd filled his evening with. Looking down at her, his curious expression turned to shock.

"Lady Capell, I was not expecting you. Please, do come in."

Clearly aware of her precarious position, arriving at his doorstep on the known bachelor street of London, he quickly ushered her inside and helped her with her cloak. Philippa was somewhat bemused to see him acting as a butler, but either he did not have one or the man was not currently on duty. She had no idea whether or not that was usual for the bachelors who inhabited Jermyn Street. Perhaps none of them had butlers late at night. It would certainly help with discretion.

"What can I do for you, my lady?" Conyngham asked, turning to face her now that her cloak was taken care of. His eyes roved appreciatively over the lowcut navy blue gown she and Katherine had picked out. It was a flattering gown that was among the most easily removed of her wardrobe.

Now that the moment was upon her though, Philippa found her mouth had gone dry. She had never had to proposition a gentleman before. For some reason she had expected Conyngham to just *know* what she wanted.

After all, he had been pursuing her, had he not? And he did have a bet with Everett, did he not?

The reminder of the bet made both her courage and her temper flare, and she lifted her chin. "I want to be pleasured until I cannot see straight," she said brazenly. "I hear you may be able to help me with that."

Interest immediately glinted in his eyes, but he did not step forward the way she expected. "I would be very happy to help you, my lady. Might I inquire, though, why me?"

"Why not you?" Philippa immediately retorted, her stomach tightening with anxiety.

"I am, shall we say, experienced when it comes to women and pleasure." He lifted his hand to brush back a strand of hair from her cheek. A small frisson of pleasure went through her at his touch, but nothing compared to when Everett had done something similar. Conyngham's lips curved in a knowing smile. "You are attracted to me, but not so much that I would have expected you to appear on my doorstep. Especially not given some of your other options . . . most women take weeks to tire of Mr. Horn's particular fetish."

A blush bloomed on her cheeks at his knowledge, which she knew was a guess, but which she had just confirmed with her reaction. For a wild moment she had thought he was referring to Everett, but of course he could not have known about the events of the past two days. "Perhaps I need something . . . more."

Which was very true. Mr. Horn was skilled at what he did, but Philippa wanted a man inside of her. On top of her. She had thought that man would be Everett. Since that was now impossible, she would take his rival to bed instead.

Conyngham grinned widely, taking her into his arms and pulling himself toward her. "Well then, my lady, I am very happy to oblige."

His lips were firm, the kiss skillfully practiced, and Philippa's body responded with interest, even as her heart regretted that such a lovely kiss did not affect her the same way Everett's had. But the magic she had felt kissing him had clearly been all on her own side. At least now, here, she knew that she and Conyngham felt the same way about each other. They were attracted to each other. She neither needed nor wanted anything more.

As the kiss deepened, she could feel her arousal growing. Slowly. Nothing like the rush from kissing Everett, but certainly more than enough if she could only stop thinking about him. She ran her hands down Conyngham's broad chest, shivering as his grip tightened on her. Concentrating on the purely physical sensations now rushing through her, everything else began to fade. His kiss deepened, his hands roaming down to her bottom and squeezing the soft flesh, making her squirm. She could feel his cock hardening against her, thick and long, his hips flexing so that it rubbed against her stomach through their clothing.

The little itch between her legs began to throb, her body heating with interest.

When Conyngham ended the kiss, she was breathing hard. The feeling was rather familiar. This was very much how her husband had made her feel whenever he'd visited her bed.

Hot. Itchy. Physically needy. The desire was there, even if more intimate emotions were not.

"This way, my lady," he said, his lips curving with a smile that could only be called triumphant.

Her heart panged a little, because she had to wonder if some of his triumph was from winning his bet with Ev—with Hartington. Blast, she had been thinking of him by his Christian name again. She must stop that. And she must stop thinking of the bet. It was meaningless to her, other than ensuring Hartington lost it.

With that in mind, as soon as Conyngham escorted her into his bedroom, she fairly launched herself into his arms, determined not to think about Hartington or the bet, or even *think* at all for one more moment. The force with which she moved was so great that Conyngham stumbled back momentarily, but he righted them quickly enough, swinging her around so he could lead her toward the bed. Her side of the kiss became almost frantic as she tugged at the buttons on his shirt, while his own hands were busy divesting her of her clothing as well. He was much better at undressing her than the other way round, and her gown was soon on the floor, while his shirt was open but still tucked into his trousers.

He was well built, with wiry, dark hairs covering his chest and trailing down the center of his stomach and into his pants. She stroked her fingers over the happy little trail and then dipped them under the hem and to touch the velvety soft knob of his cock. Conyngham groaned and Philippa giggled. He lifted her up off of her feet. She wrapped her legs around him, her smooth bare skin rubbing against his upper body, the hairs on his chest stimulating her hard nipples and exciting her further. Her insides ached to be filled.

The bed was soft and he pressed down on top of her,

pushing her into the mattress. The feel of a man's weight above her, surrounding her, was wonderful. Spreading her legs wider, she wrapped her ankles around the backs of his thighs, pulling him close.

"Slow down, my lady," he murmured, nuzzling her neck with his lips. "I promise there's no rush."

"I want you inside me," she countered, wriggling beneath him and groaning when his hips moved away instead. She soon found herself flipped over onto her stomach, his hands underneath her, squeezing her breasts. The fabric of his pants rubbed against her bottom, the rigid bulge of his cock rubbing up the center of her cheeks. He chuckled darkly and pinched her nipples, which made her pussy clench at the pleasurable zing of pain. The tiny buds throbbed between his fingers and she moaned, pushing herself up onto her elbows to give him better access. The new position pressed her more firmly against his groin. She gasped as the bulge of his cock settled between her cheeks more deeply, rubbing over sensitive areas she had not known she had.

He pinched her nipples again, tugging and twisting them, and Philippa cried out, arching her back.

"Please," she begged, pressing deliberately back against him.

Chuckling again, he gave her breasts one last caress and then slid his hands down her sides, cupping her hips. "Stay just like that, my lady."

While his tone made it sound like a request, it was definitely an order, and Philippa obeyed. Although she did peek over her shoulder to see what he was doing. His gaze was trained on her upturned bottom, the expression on his face full of desire and heat, like he was looking at a tempting treat that he could scarcely believe was his to devour. That expression went a long way toward soothing the small worry that he only wanted her for the bet, like Ev—like Hartington. Especially when Conyngham's gaze raised, meeting hers, and he blinked as if surprised to see her looking back at him. The way he had been looking at her was clearly not for show.

Grinning at her, he reached down to caress her pussy, and Philippa gasped as his fingers stroked her sensitive folds. Her head dropped back down in front of her as her arms quaked. He dipped his fingers into her, making her mewl, because it was so close to what she wanted, but not quite.

Then his fingers retreated and swirled upward, higher, pressing against a most forbidden spot. Philippa gasped, jerking forward, but she did not stop him. It did not feel . . . bad. Just different. Almost good. She pressed her burning face against the bed.

Was this something her husband had wanted from his mistresses?

She would have done this for him.

Conyngham's finger pushed inside of her, and she clenched hard around him, trying to force him back out.

"Have you ever had a cock here, my lady?" he asked, his finger probing deeper, invading her in a shockingly intimate manner that burned slightly as her muscles stretched.

"A *cock*? *There*?" She asked the question faintly, somewhat aghast. Perhaps *that* was what Clarence had wanted from his mistresses, something that he had not expected his wife to provide.

"Apparently not." Another dark chuckle, his finger

twisting inside of her, and then she felt his cock sliding through her wet folds.

Slowly he pushed into her, groaning at her tightness, while she whimpered and wriggled at the utterly delicious sensation of being filled. *Yes*, her body whispered, *this is what I needed.*

Philippa gave herself over to the sensations: the hard cock that began with slow, steady strokes, while the forbidden pleasure of his finger in her bottom ignited a wholly different kind of fervor. Her nipples brushing against the sheets of his bed. The way his thick cock felt, pushing back and forth inside of her, stimulating parts of her that had not been touched in far too long.

With him behind her, he became a faceless man, he could have been anyone . . . and if the face she pictured was all too familiar, if the hair was darker, the eyes brighter . . . well, no one would know but her.

As her passion climbed higher, his finger slid away from her bottom, leaving it feeling oddly empty, so he could grip her hips and ride her in earnest. Philippa cried out as his thrusts became harder, more forceful, each one pressing against that secret spot inside of her that bloomed with pleasure every time it was touched. Her fingers and toes curled, heat licking along her skin, until she screamed with ecstasy, so lost in her own climax that she barely noticed when Conyngham withdrew and spurted his seed across her back and bottom.

CHAPTER SIXTEEN

EARLY MORNING, THE DAY AFTER HIS MONU-
mental mistake with Pippa, Everett was at her front door
feeling very much like a penitent at church. He was there
to fully confess his wrongdoings, profess the truth of
his emotions, and—hopefully—receive forgiveness and
salvation.

After returning to London late last night, he'd walked
by her house to see the lights out and the curtains shut.
Rather than pounding on her door so late at night, he
thought it better to give her more time and a good night's
rest before pounding on her door early in the morning. He
had spent a sleepless night trying to plan out exactly what
to say to her, how to explain himself in a way that did not
make him sound like a complete ass.

In the end, he had come to the realization that he *had*
been a complete ass, and he should probably acknowledge
that and apologize profusely rather than undermine his
apology by trying to justify the unjustifiable.

To his surprise, the door swung open even before he
could knock, and it was not a butler standing there to
greet him, nor Pippa, but Pippa's companion Katherine,

fixing him with a glare that would do the devil proud. But Everett had spent the night facing his own demons, so he straightened his spine, although he kept his voice respectful and humble as he made his request.

"I would like to speak with Lady Capell, please."

Something flashed in her eyes, and her lips firmed before curving into a smile that was not really a smile at all. "Lady Capell is not here." She said it triumphantly, although Everett did not understand why at first. "I believe she spent the evening settling your *bet* with Lord Conyngham."

She spat the word "bet" at him, like a curse, and truly it was.

Anger roared up inside of him, jealousy flaring . . . and it was just as quickly dampened by the sad, sick knowledge that it was his own damn fault. Perhaps he even should have anticipated such a move on Pippa's part. It made sense, did it not? He had hurt her, again, and so she had taken the only route where she thought it would be possible to hurt him—his pride and his pocketbook.

It would not have even occurred to her that she might have been able to hurt his heart. She did not believe she had access to it. And why would she, after all that Everett had done?

Roger had been right.

This was his comeuppance.

Yet . . .

A tiny spark of hope kindled.

If the bet was over with, if he'd already lost, then perhaps . . .

She would have to believe him now, wouldn't she?

The sound of horse's hooves clattering against the

street, pulling a creaking carriage to a halt in front of the house, had Everett turning. The carriage was black, discreet. He was not entirely surprised to see Pippa when the door opened, stepping down from the interior before looking up at her doorstep.

Her lips parted in surprise when she saw him, and she went pink with embarrassment and then pale with real-ization and then very bright red as her anger came back to her. She lifted her chin in challenge and began to march toward him, a defiant look in her eye.

Everett stalked toward her as well, feeling Miss Parrish's eyes on his back.

Stomping up to him, Pippa came to a halt. "I regret to inform you that you have lost your bet with Lord Conyn-gham, my lord."

"I do not regret it," Everett said savagely, and Pippa's bright blue eyes widened with shock when he caught her about the neck, his other hand going to her waist, and pulled her in for a rough kiss. It was not a long one, for he ended it before she could push him away, but it was quick and thorough and claiming. The utter confusion in her eyes when he pulled away cut him to the quick, but he knew he needed to retreat and collect himself. Seeing her fresh from Conyngham's bed hurt. He would not deny it, even if he did hope it would ultimately be to his advantage. "Now you will have to believe me. I love you, Pippa. And I mean to have you as my wife."

With that, he released her and stormed off. It might be very early in the morning, but he needed a stiff drink.

Lips bruised and emotions shaken from that harsh,

sudden kiss, Philippa stared at Ev—*Hartington's* back as he quick-stepped down the street away from her.

"What on earth . . .?" Katherine breathed the question from beside her, arm hooking around her in support, which Philippa desperately needed. "Did he really just say that?"

"Yes . . ." Philippa was utterly flabbergasted. "Yes he did. But . . . why?"

He was not supposed to want her any longer. He was supposed to be angry at the loss of his bet. Defeated, knowing all his hard work in wooing her and pretending to love her had been for naught. Certainly he was not supposed to still be proclaiming that he had any feelings for her.

She did not understand.

It did not make sense.

Not unless . . .

But no.

That was impossible.

Wasn't it?

"Men are impossible," Olivia whispered sagely, shaking her head.

Truly, teatime was not the proper venue for confiding in her friend, but it was the first chance Philippa had since they had returned from Beaufort's house party.

At least they had managed a table together—just her, Olivia, and Katherine for now. Lady Brookes was still greeting some of the fashionably late guests, which gave them some coverage for their conversation.

Philippa just had to shake her head and laugh, though. "When has Francis ever been impossible?"

"He's impossible because he is far too good at always doing the right thing," Olivia said, rolling her eyes. "It is extremely annoying."

"Only to you," Philippa teased her. Then she sighed. "I do not know what to do, though. It has been two days and he has not sought me out. Am I supposed to go to him now?"

"Certainly not." Olivia shook her head in unison with Katherine, who looked relieved that Olivia agreed with her assessment. "He has not even apologized yet, has he?"

"No, no apology, but—"

"No," Olivia said firmly, giving Philippa a stern look. "When you receive an apology, then you may make the next move, and not before."

Sighing, Philippa took a sip of her tea, letting the smooth flavor roll over her tongue and soothe her. "I know you are right, I just . . ."

"You feel guilty because you thought he had been lying to you about everything, and it turned out he had only been lying to you about some things," Katherine interjected. "But telling the truth about some things still does not make up for the lies."

As far as Philippa knew, Katherine had still not forgiven Sunderland either, and the dark look in her eyes made it seem unlikely that she would any time soon. She was far more stubborn than Philippa was—although, of course, she did not have the kind of history that Philippa did with Everett either.

"Everyone lies." Olivia sipped her tea. "The question is, what do they lie for? Who does their lie serve? Who does it damage? And is it forgivable?"

Katherine huffed. "People should just tell the truth."

"Like how you told Sunderland you are in love with him?"

To Philippa's surprise, Katherine turned beet red. "That is not . . . I . . . it is not the same."

"To me, no. But you do not seem to agree, as you have not told him the truth about your feelings for him. You are holding Sunderland to a different standard than you are holding yourself." Olivia smiled sagely when her words clearly hit the mark and Katherine shrank in on herself a bit, frowning as she thought over Olivia's observation.

"What about me?" Philippa asked, curious what her friend would say. "Am I holding Hartington to a different standard than myself?" She knew some would say so, especially as she had been enjoying herself with other gentlemen while insisting Everett remain celibate.

If he had been staying celibate . . .

Which, if he truly only wanted her for a bet, he might not have. But he seemed to mean that he loved her and wanted to marry her. Blast, she was so confused.

"No," Olivia said slowly. "If anything, you seem to be holding him to the same standard you used to hold for yourself. I assume that if you truly decide to give him a chance to court you, you will end your time as a merry widow?"

"Of course," Philippa said instantly.

Her friend shrugged. "Considering the number of hoops he had you jumping through when he said he loved you before, I do not blame you for not leaping at a second chance with him. Nor should you have changed *your* plans just because he wanted that chance. What . . ."

Her voice trailed off and her eyes widened, something behind Philippa catching her attention. Somewhat alarmed, Philippa turned to see what the distraction was, and was shocked when she saw Everett and Lord Sunderland greeting Lady Brookes.

Unmarried gentlemen of Everett's age and stature did not attend afternoon teas unless they were bride-hunting. No, they did not attend unless they were *publicly* in search of a bride.

Conversation around the room petered out as more than one lady realized exactly who had just entered their arena—and what it meant. Lord Sunderland's appearance would garner interest too, but not nearly as much as Everett's once the gossips realized he was there.

"Oh my," murmured Olivia. "This is certainly going to be interesting."

Gaze moving around the room, Everett's eyes lit up as soon as they met Philippa's. Without missing a beat, he began to move straight for her. Whispers sprang up as quickly as the conversation had initially died. The *ton* had not been blind to the future duke's interest in the Dowager Countess of Essex, and his appearance at an afternoon tea with his attention fixed upon her might as well have been an engagement announcement.

Philippa was torn between wanting to swoon at the romance of such a gesture or strangle him.

Attending a ladies' afternoon tea was daunting enough, but not nearly as much as approaching Pippa's table where she sat with Lady Hertford and Miss Parrish on either side of her like twin guardian angels. At least Miss Parrish's darkest glare was reserved for Sunderland and not for himself.

He would have liked to have come flanked by two

friends as well, but Roger had flat out refused to cross the threshold of an afternoon tea.

At least Lady Hertford was not glaring at him with the same force as Miss Parrish's ire, although the warning in her eyes was clear.

Pippa was his main concern, though, and the expression on her face was unreadable. The blank social mask that had descended over her features was better than outright hostility, he supposed. Still, it was not exactly encouraging either.

"Ladies," he said with a bow, echoed by Sunderland. Everett sat across from Pippa, while Sunderland daringly took the seat next to Miss Parrish. Her lips pursed, but she glanced at Olivia and the intensity of her glare softened just a touch.

"Lord Hartington. Lord Sunderland." Pippa nodded politely. "Would you care for some tea?"

The social banalities were tedious but necessary. Everett pushed down his impatience as he and Sunderland accepted her offer and talked about the weather. He was all too aware of how eagerly the tables closest to them were listening—and it did not escape his notice that more than one lady found a convenient excuse to walk by. Several of them stopped to "just have a word" with Pippa or Lady Hertford.

After what felt like an interminable wait, but was really only about a quarter of an hour, their neighbors had mostly lost interest in their banal conversation and there was a lull in visitors.

"Lady Essex, would you care for a turn about the garden?" he asked, keeping his tone light. He did not want to pressure her, but he desperately wished for some time alone. Both Olivia and Katherine gave him warning glances now, which he ignored as best he could.

"Why yes, thank you, that would be lovely," she replied, and the tightness in Everett's chest unclenched.

"Perhaps I could escort *you*, Miss Parrish," Sunderland said, giving the lady his most charming smile. Before she could refuse him outright, he turned his head to the marchioness. "And Lady Hertford, too, of course."

"Of course," Lady Hertford said dryly, but she smiled at him. "I would love a walkabout."

"Then I suppose I would too," Miss Parrish said. It was not the most encouraging acceptance, but Sunderland grinned widely. Everett silently wished his friend good luck. They were both sure to need it.

CHAPTER SEVENTEEN

WALKING OUT INTO THE GARDEN WITH Everett, Philippa did not know what to say to him. Too many questions crowded her mind, all with seemingly equal importance.

Everett took the reins of the conversation anyway, as he often did.

"I owe you a multitude of apologies," he said quietly, not that anyone could overhear them. Sunderland was speaking with Katherine and Olivia in normal tones, yet they were far enough behind Everett and Philippa that their words were muddled. "I did not think about how you might perceive the bet, that it might taint your view of my feelings for you."

She snorted. It was an incredibly uncouth, unladylike sound, but it happened before she could stop it.

Grinding to a halt, she turned to face him, pulling her hand from his arm and putting her fists on her hips. "Did you think at *all?*"

"No," he admitted, rubbing his hand over his face. "As usual I was a proper dunderhead. I honestly have no excuse for my behavior. I . . . I thought I had a better control of my pride after all these years, but it turns out I did not. I realize that now. I made the bet before I knew you were back in London, and when I realized you were the chosen woman, I did not want to admit to my friends what you meant to me, especially if you refused my suit.

"I wanted to impress them, win the bet, *and* win you. I was not thinking about how you might feel, knowing about the bet. I was only thinking of myself and what I wanted." He stepped forward, reaching to take her hand in his, and she allowed him to do so. "I am changing that now. I do not care if the world knows that I am courting you and you refuse me. I do not care that I lost the bet. Well, I care in that I am jealous as hell of Conyngham, but I do not care about the bet itself.

"I've made mistakes, Pippa. So many. But I want to make them right. And I want you. I want those two things more than I want anything else. But if I can only have the one, then I will accept that."

His fingers pressed against hers, and she stared back at him. Everything about his expression, his body language, screamed his open sincerity. He was completely in earnest.

Give him another chance.

The voice whispered in the back of her mind, seductive and appealing. It would be a foolish thing to do, would it not?

And yet . . .

He truly was risking everything. His pride. His reputation. The gossip had already been swirling, and after coming to the tea today and taking her about the garden, it was going to be completely out of control. If she rejected him out of hand, after so public a declaration, it would be the talk of the Season.

Every part of her body yearned to step forward into his arms, to say yes, to kiss him. To see if his kiss still affected her so strongly. She could not, of course.

Not here.

She did not even know if she should. Though . . . he had passed every test she had set him. Even those she did not realize she was assigning to him. Like Hercules, he had done things she thought were impossible. Accepted that she was exploring pleasure with other lovers. Taken no new lover himself. Put his reputation on the line to save hers. Publicly defied his parents' wishes.

"We should go somewhere else." She blurted out the words before she could think too hard about them.

Everett's brow wrinkled in confusion. "What?"

"Somewhere else," she repeated. "Somewhere more private."

Although he still appeared confused, he did not argue. "Now?"

"Now."

Deciding it was best not to question his good fortune, Everett quickly spun a tale for Lady Brookes and swept Pippa right out of the tea. Neither of her friends seemed particularly happy to see her go, but she did not give them a chance to argue with her either. He was surprised to see that Miss Parrish seemed to have softened considerably toward Sunderland.

So perhaps he was not wrong to feel hopeful.

Giving his driver the instruction to take them to Pippa's home, Everett joined her in the carriage. With the curtain drawn for privacy, the lighting was dim and the air slightly stuffy, but neither of those things bothered him much. He was too surprised and glad to have Pippa there with him.

He was also at a bit of a loss at the turn of events, which had not been in his plan.

"Did . . . was there something you wished to talk about?" he asked cautiously.

"No."

The answer did not surprise him, but what followed next certainly did. She leaned forward, reaching out with her hands, and grabbed him by the lapels, pulling him in for a kiss. The lurching motion of the carriage as she yanked him forward set him completely off balance and he practically tumbled into her.

Her kiss was eager, even as they awkwardly sorted out their limbs. The brief tussle ended with Everett on the seat and Pippa on his lap with her legs and skirts over his thighs. Despite his confusion, his cock was already hardening under her bottom as she continued to kiss him.

"What is happening?" he asked, pulling her away from him. "I do not object on principle, but I am not sure I understand."

"I have decided to consider your suit," Pippa said, her manner formally haughty. Under other circumstances, Everett might have laughed. Right now he was too delighted.

"You have?"

"I have," she answered softly, leaning more fully against him. Gentle fingers stroked his cheek, her own cheek resting against his head—which put *his* head nearly on her bosom. "I can only think of one reason you would still be pursuing me in such a manner . . . but Everett. Do not break my heart again. There will not be a third chance."

"I will not need it," he said fiercely, tightening his arms around her. If he had his way, he would never let her go again.

They almost fell getting out of the carriage. Lips swollen from Everett's kisses, giggling like a mischievous child, she managed to get them into the house and up to her room before throwing herself at him again.

His kisses truly were different, and she was on fire for him.

While her body might have been satisfied by the touch of any man she was attracted to, it was not the same as touching the man she truly wanted. Who truly wanted her. Strangely, despite everything, she now felt more secure in Everett's regard for her than before.

Or perhaps it was not so strange. Everything he had done in the past weeks, other than the bet, had publicly tied him to her. After today, no one could doubt it. This was not like before when he had wanted to keep his courtship a "private matter." It certainly had nothing to do with the bet, since that had ended. For the first time, perhaps ever, she felt truly assured of his feelings for her.

And she wanted him to know she felt the same.

She would not say that she had loved him still, after all this time, but she could not deny that he had rekindled her old feelings.

"Pippa . . ." He murmured the nickname as though it were an endearment, and perhaps it was. She whimpered as his lips passed over her neck, her skin tingling in their wake. When he filled his hands with her breasts, she moaned, pulling more frantically at the buttons on his waistcoat.

She wanted to feel him against her. To touch him bare skin to bare skin. To have him inside of her. The craving was as much for intimacy with him as anything else. All of the physical needs were intensified by the warmth of her emotion for him. She could swear it felt better when he touched her than when anyone else had, and not because he was more skilled.

Just because it was him.

When his head dipped down to her breast, sucking her nipple into his mouth, she cried out as her core throbbed with need. Clutching at his hair, she held him to her breast, pressing her thighs together to ease the ache between them. Fabric ripped as she tore one of his shirt-sleeves in her haste.

"Oh dear . . ."

Everett snorted. "Do not concern yourself with that, darling. I am not."

Quickly, he shucked off his .top before finishing unlacing her dress. He was well muscled, with dark curls of hair spread across his chest. A narrow strip of hair below his belly button disappeared into the top of his trousers. Clearly, he did not use any padding to enhance his shoulders or muscles—he had no need to.

The fabric of her dress slid from her body and then he made quick work of her corset and chemise, so that she was entirely naked before him. Before he could say anything, she dropped to her knees, reaching for the buttons on his trousers. His cock was straining against the flap and her mouth watered in anticipation.

"Pippa . . ." His voice was hoarse, but he did not stop her as she released his cock. Long, thick, with a dark pink head that had a glossy drop of fluid at its tip. It stood up long and straight from the coarse curls round its base, jerking slightly as she studied it. Not so different from other men's, and yet it felt different to gaze upon his.

Her fingers wrapped around the thick shaft, feeling the veins and bumps, his skin so soft with the hard core beneath. Bending her head, she guided his cock to her lips. The only other man she had ever taken in her mouth was her husband, and she certainly had not craved the taste of him like this. It had been interesting, more a matter of curiosity and wanting to please her husband. Now, though, she sucked on the thick length of Everett's cock like she was worshiping it.

"Bloody hell, Pippa."

He would never have thought such a thing before this moment, but perhaps Pippa's experience with gentlemen was not all bad. A virgin would certainly never have thought to do such a thing as sucking his cock, nor would she have been so very good at it. Pippa was eager, her fist wrapped round the base, head bobbing back and forth, while her tongue swirled over his sensitive skin.

Burying his fingers in her hair, curving them against her scalp, he groaned as he thrust forward into the heated confines of her mouth. She felt so bloody good. Staring down at her, he memorized the sight of her lips stretched around his cock, the way her cheeks hollowed as she sucked him deeper, the glazed look of pleasure in her eyes as she bent to her task.

The only thing he didn't like was that he could not touch her the way he wanted to. She was completely naked and on her knees before him, leaving him torn between taking his time using her mouth or exploring her body the way he dreamed of.

When her other hand came up to cup his sack, gently squeezing his balls, the jolt of ecstasy was enough to make up his mind for him. He quickly pulled back before he could lose complete control like a callow youth. Pippa made a noise of protest, but he bodily picked her up and tossed her onto the bed.

"You are far too good at that," he growled at her, crawling onto the bed after her. She was sprawled, thighs spread slightly apart, propped up on her elbows to look at him. "And I am not ready for this to be over yet."

Understanding made her eyes widen, and then he scooped up her legs and pushed them up toward her body, spreading them wide. She'd had her turn to taste him. Now it was his.

The slightly salty-sweet flavor of Everett's cock lingered on Philippa's tongue. Kneeling before him, seeing his expression of awe and lust when she'd sucked on him, had aroused her far more than she'd thought possible. Her pussy felt swollen and sensitive from her rising desire, and when his tongue delved between the folds, her hips bucked.

Palms flat against the backs of her thighs, he held her firmly open, in a far more intimate and forceful manner than any of her other lovers had before. If he was not as skillful as the dedicated Mr. Horn, Philippa truly did not notice, because it did not matter. She moaned, clutching his hair as he licked and sucked at her tender flesh, sending her passionate need climbing higher.

Her body tingled and throbbed, the sensations winding tighter and tighter inside of her.

"Everett . . ." Just saying his name aloud as he pleasured her increased her arousal for some reason. "Oh Everett . . ."

Before she could reach her pinnacle, though, her legs were dropped down. And then he was on top of her.

Hot.

Heavy.

Hard.

His mouth closed over hers, swallowing her scream of passion as he thrust inside of her.

With their flavors mingling on her tongue, her body stretching open to take him inside, and his weight pressing her down into the bed, Philippa felt almost faint from the sensations sweeping through her. Bedding him did feel different from other men. The emotions she felt for him amplified the physical pleasure, making everything feel more intense.

When his body came together with hers, it was like he fit perfectly inside of her, his groin rubbing pleasurably against her sensitive flesh, his cock snugly nestled inside of her.

It felt more than good, it felt right.

And then he began to move.

Long, hard thrusts drew moans from her lips. She squirmed beneath him, muscles clenching around him, as each stroke of his cock added another dollop of pleasure to her hoard. Raking her fingernails down his chest, she arched her back, wrapping her legs around him, rubbing herself against him.

Their movements became more frantic, and he tore his mouth away from hers, no longer able to kiss her as their ecstasy climbed higher.

The room echoed with their cries and gasps. Everett pounded between her thighs, his body braced by his forearms on either side of her, caging her beneath him while his cock drew the most delicious sensations from her quivering channel.

"Everett!" She fairly screamed his name when his cock drove into her, hitting her in the exact right spot to send her soaring. Her arms and legs were wrapped around him as she sobbed out her ecstasy, the rapture winding through her entire body and exploding like little fireworks all along her nerves.

It was only as her climax wound down that she realized he had not reached his pinnacle yet. Still throbbing and tingling, she whimpered when she felt how hard he was still inside of her.

"Will you take me back in your mouth?" he asked, pressing his forehead against hers, his cock pulsing inside of her. His voice was hoarse, tense, and she realized how close he was to his own release.

And what his question meant.

Her body flushed with heat.

"Yes," she whispered.

Everett moved so quickly. One moment he was still inside of her, the next he was straddling her chest, one hand on his cock, the other on his headboard as he leaned over her. Philippa wrapped her arms around the backs of his thighs, her hands curving over to the front, as she lifted her head to suck him back into her mouth.

He thrust in deep, once . . . twice . . . and then he groaned with pleasure.

Rubbing her tongue along the underside of his cock, she could feel every pulse of his climax before hot liquid spilled into her mouth. The taste of their combined pleasure flooded her mouth, and Everett groaned as he tightened his grip on the headboard, hips pumping softly.

Philippa swallowed convulsively, sucking until he sighed with completion and all of his muscles relaxed.

Curled up around a naked Pippa, Everett stroked her shoulder. He still could not believe how the events of the afternoon had completely turned. What he did know was that he wanted to stay just like this, forever. He wanted every night with Pippa and every morning, and every time he could get in between.

She stirred slightly against him and said something so softly he could not hear her.

"What, love?" he asked, nuzzling the back of her neck.

"It's different with you." She was still speaking softly, but just loud enough to be audible.

"What is?"

"Everything."

For a long moment, Everett considered her words.

"Yes. It is."

CHAPTER EIGHTEEN

ENGAGED.

To Everett Cavendish, Marquess of Hartington and future Duke of Devonshire, no less.

At one point, she had been sure that was her future. Then, for a long time, sure that it never would be.

Now it was her reality.

She was walking into one of the premiere balls of the Season on his arm. It was the stuff she'd dreamed of years ago. Now, she felt so anxious she could barely stand it.

When she had imagined this moment as a younger woman, she'd had no knowledge of heartbreak or the cruelty of the *ton*. She had never thought there was an obstacle they could not overcome. Now she knew differently.

For the past few days they had shunned the world outside, and Philippa had preferred it that way. Olivia and Francis had come for dinner, Everett's friend Roger had visited them, and Katherine had been in the house of course, although she was more than a little distracted by Sunderland. He was the most frequent visitor to the house after Everett.

But as Everett only left to change his clothes, that was not showing a lack of commitment on Sunderland's part. Philippa was happy that Katherine had reconciled with her beau, as she would have felt awfully guilty if they had not.

Existing in their own little bubble had been lovely, but invitations were piling up, the others reported that the gossip was swinging wildly out of hand, and Everett's mother was going on a tear across Society in an effort to damage Philippa's reputation. So they had no choice but to face the *ton*.

Pippa had written her father and her son-in-law to inform them she had accepted Everett's proposal and would soon be the new Marchioness of Hartington rather than the Dowager Countess of Essex. This morning their engagement announcement had appeared in the paper. Tonight, they were making their first public appearance as a couple at Lady Jersey's ball. Everyone who was anyone would be in attendance, especially as Olivia, Roger, and Sunderland had taken pains to spread the news that they would be making an appearance.

The long line of carriages they'd waited through had attested to the crush.

Whispers had surrounded them from the moment they'd left their conveyance, all through the receiving line up to their hosts. Lady Jersey's eyes gleamed with pleasure when she saw them. An incorrigible gossip, she would be thrilled that they chose her ball to make their debut. Which, of course, was part of why they'd chosen it. Having the influential lady happy with them could only help.

"Lord Hartington. Lady Essex. I am so very pleased to see you," Lady Jersey said, practically preening as they approached her. "Congratulations on your very happy news. I assume the banns will be forthcoming?"

"Starting this Sunday," Everett reassured her, bowing over her hand and then taking Philippa's on his arm again. He angled a look at Philippa, playing it up like a lovesick swain, and she nearly ruined his efforts by giggling at how foppish he looked.

It suited their purposes very well, though, and she managed to simper back up at him, much to Lady Jersey's clear delight. She was rumored to be a romantic at heart, and it appeared as though the rumors were true.

"It is a love match, then?" Lady Jersey asked, nodding sagely. "I thought as much, what with your parents' disapproval." It was clear she was fishing for more gossip.

"They will learn to love Pippa as I do," Everett said firmly. Philippa's stomach churned with tension, but she beamed up at him, more than a little soothed by his public declaration.

His parents were going to be a sore subject for Pippa, it was clear. Not that he blamed her for that. Even though he had taken steps to enable them to live independently from his parents, he still felt a high amount of anxiety and guilt over defying them so openly. It was not as if they had been terrible to him, after all, but the time had come to cut their strings on his life.

What he wanted for his future and what they wanted were two very different visions, and he had already sacrificed his for theirs once. Thankfully, he now had a second chance at the future he desired, and he was not going to make the same mistake again.

His life was his to live. Not theirs.

Moving past Lady Jersey, Pippa clung to his arm as they entered the ballroom. Everett doubted anyone looking at her would know she was trembling. Her head was held high, chin almost defiantly pointed in the air.

As soon as they walked in, he felt her relax, and he looked in the same direction she was. The Marquess and Marchioness of Hertford were there, waiting for them with Sunderland, Miss Parrish, and Roger beside them, as planned. They were there to bolster Everett and Pippa if it became necessary. Everett smiled.

Unfortunately they did not make it halfway to their group when the last person Everett wanted to see slid in front of them, her eyes so narrowed he could barely see the color. Two spots of red were high on her cheeks and she looked near to bursting. All the signs that his mother was about to royally lose her temper.

"You." She hissed the word at Pippa, and Everett immediately pulled his fiancée back, stepping forward to shield her from his mother's fury.

"Mother." The word was acknowledgement and warning all in one. The whispers around them had died out as quickly as they had started, everyone watching to see what would happen next. Out of the corner of his eye, Everett could see the Hertfords and others moving toward them, but they were still too far away to help buffer the scene his mother clearly wanted to make. Everett kept his voice as low as he could. "If you force my hand, you will not like the choice I make. I love Pippa and she is going to be my wife. I hope you can be happy for us."

Pure fury flashed across her features and Everett realized in that moment she was already too far gone. She did not care about his happiness, she only cared about what *she* wanted. A deep sadness washed over him at the proof standing right in front of him.

Whatever vitriol might have next spilled from her mouth, he would never know, because a deep, happy voice came from behind him, cutting her off before she could utter a single word.

"Lady Essex, my dear. Best wishes for you and the lucky Lord Hartington." Turning, Everett was taken aback to see the Duke of Beaufort standing with Pippa's hands in his, kissing her cheeks, while his own father stood next to Beaufort silently and quietly fuming. Beaufort glanced at Everett's father. "I had asked her to marry me as well, did I tell you? But I do not blame her for choosing the younger, handsomer man."

Beaufort bellowed a laugh while Everett's father smiled weakly, and the number of whispers sweeping across the ballroom noticeably increased.

Two dukes had been vying for Lady Essex's hand. That Everett was not yet a duke did not matter to them, they all knew he would be one day. The gossips were going to be out of control tomorrow.

Glancing over his shoulder at his mother, Everett was pleased to see that she no longer looked like a tempest about to break. If anything, she had shrunk in on herself. They could both sense the volatile mood of their audience shifting. While the *ton* might have been intrigued by an ugly scene between the current Duchess of Devonshire and her son, they were far more enamored of a love triangle between two dukes.

Stirring up a confrontation now, spoiling the romance of the moment, would do nothing but stir up sympathies for Everett and Pippa.

After all, a rival duke vying for Pippa's affections *and* parents who opposed the match? The *ton* would be hoping for an elopement to Gretna Green next. Truthfully, Everett would not be averse to giving it to them, but Pippa wanted a proper wedding with the banns read and the ceremony in St. George's, and he wanted Pippa to have whatever she wanted.

Her hands in Curtis's, she could have hugged the man if it would not have caused a complete scandal. While he had not been upset when she had informed him she would not be able to marry him, she had not expected this level of public support from him. In fact, she had been rather dreading facing him again, having accepted Everett's suit so soon after she had refused his.

That he was making it nearly impossible for Everett's parents to be anything other than supportive, or else risk the *ton*'s displeasure, made her even more grateful to him.

Looking up and past her, his smile widened. "Congratulations, Hartington. I am sure you know what a treasure you have here." Beaufort released Philippa to shake hands with Everett.

Philippa was relieved when Olivia and Katherine wedged their way through the crowd, finally reaching her side so she was not left facing Everett's father alone. Clearing his throat nervously, Everett's father adjusted his cravat and gave her a nod of acknowledgement.

"I ah . . . I suppose I should welcome you to the family." The duke stumbled slightly over his words, and his smile was very strained, but Philippa chose to be gracious and pretend she thought he meant it.

"Thank you, your grace," she said, dipping into a curtsey. "I am truly honored."

Thankfully she was not required to say anything more, because Curtis and Everett had finished greeting each other. Everett moved to her side, his steady presence everything she needed to remain stalwart in the face of his parents. While there was a wistful part of her that wished he had been this way the first time round, she also thought perhaps it had turned out for the better.

Both of them had grown during their time apart, and she liked herself better now than she had back then. The confidence she now had, her stronger backbone—she would not give either of those things up for the world. She certainly did not have any regrets over the adventures she had undertaken this Season. Now she understood that his original betrayal had nothing to do with any short-comings on her own part. Neither did Clarence's. Perhaps Clarence had been looking for the emotions, the love, she had found with Everett. Though she had given Clarence her body, she had withheld her heart. Thinking about his philandering no longer hurt, and she knew her second marriage would be far more successful and satisfying than her first because there was a foundation of love.

As her friends and the rest of the *ton* surged forward to add their congratulations and well wishes to the Duke of Beaufort's, the Duke and Duchess of Devonshire melted away into the crowd.

Certainly it was noticed that the duchess did not address her, but since the duke had done so, the only words Philippa heard on the subject were snide comments about the duchess not being able to have her way in everything. The general consensus, Olivia reported later, was that no one was particularly sorry to see the duchess taken down a peg, and they were all wildly in favor of the small taste of forbidden romance between Everett and Philippa.

Since the duke and duchess left the ball almost immediately, the focus remained on Everett and Philippa, especially when they finally took to the floor for a waltz.

Remembering that just a few weeks ago she had waltzed in his arms very much like this, hating the necessity, she could not help but smile up at him. Everett smiled back down at her, his eyes alight with happiness.

"Penny for your thoughts."

"I was just thinking about the last time we danced like this," she admitted.

"Ah yes. When I was the barely tolerable preference over Lord Shaftesbury," he teased her.

Philippa wrinkled her nose. "That man was odious." Her gaze sharpened. "By the way, do not ever think to treat me the way he does his wife. I would make sure you regret it."

"Of that, I have no doubt," Everett said, swinging her around to avoid colliding with Lord Sunderland and Katherine. His arm tightened, pulling her in closer, eyes warm with emotion. "There is no need to worry, Pippa. You are getting exactly what you wished for—a marriage with a man who loves you beyond reason and who is going to spend the rest of his life ensuring you never doubt it."

Blinking away tears, Philippa's smile felt so large that it hurt her cheeks. "I love you too, Ev."

It was the first time she had used the shortened nickname from their first romance, and Ev responded in the most scandalous way possible. Stopping dead in the middle of the floor, he pulled her in for a kiss, to the delight, shock, and titillation of the *ton*, who talked about nothing else for weeks.

CHAPTER NINETEEN

"MY WIFE." EVERETT SWUNG PIPPA OVER the threshold, grinning from ear to ear, while she laughed and clung to his neck. She beamed up at him, ethereally beautiful in her periwinkle gown with its overlay of silver and white lace, her hair spun into coils studded by diamonds. The sparkle in her eyes outdid any of the jewels in her hair or round her throat, though.

Their wedding at St. George's had been everything they wanted. The *ton* had come out in force, including his parents, who were seated in the front pew. Everett had only spoken to them once since Lady Jersey's ball, to remind them to be on their best behavior at his wedding and thereafter. Disrespect to his wife would not be tolerated. One wrong word from them and he would cut them out of his life, and the lives of any children he and Pippa would have.

Discovering that he did not need their money or anything else from them, as well as his threat about access to their future grandchildren, had apparently done the trick. His mother had even had a smile on her face, strained though it was.

But neither the ceremony nor the wedding brunch that followed filled Everett with the same sort of satisfaction he felt now, carrying his wife across the threshold of *their* home. They had not spent a night apart in weeks, but they had always been in the house she had rented, not in their home. The distinction was small, but meaningful.

This would be their first night in their home as husband and wife.

His cock was already aching to be buried inside of her and had been ever since he had put the ring on her finger that morning. Just calling her "wife" made him throb and ache.

"My husband," she responded, running her fingers through the back of his hair.

Hearing her call him that had an even more profound effect on his raging cock. With a low growl under his breath, he swung them toward the stairs and practically vaulted up to the second floor, shouldering open the door to their bedroom. By the time he got there, Pippa had already pulled off his cravat and was kissing her way down his neck, her little teeth nibbling on the sensitive skin in a manner guaranteed to drive him wild.

"Minx." Letting her legs drop, he held onto her upper body, his hands already going to work on the laces to her dress.

Making a sound halfway between a whimper and a purr, Pippa snuggled up against him and tugged the shirt from his pants. The movement rubbed against his cock and Everett groaned, pulling her more tightly against him.

Half-clothed, they tumbled onto the bed together, working to divest each other of the rest of their clothing. Caressing, kissing . . . Everett had already learned everything that Pippa liked over the past few weeks and he used it to good effort now, rousing her passion as quickly and hotly as she did his.

Her breasts were soft and plump in his hands and Everett nipped at the cherry buds of her nipples, making her gasp and writhe beneath him. Her hips canted upwards, pushing against him, legs spreading and pulling his body closer. Groaning around the mouthful of soft flesh, he rubbed the underside of his cock along the wet slit of her pussy, teasing both of them in the most delicious manner.

"Mine," he mumbled, pulling his hips back so he could thrust into her, sinking into her heat. "My wife."

Everett's words claiming her just as he entered her made Philippa feel nearly faint with desire. She cried out, clutching him, her entire body on fire. He pushed inside of her, filling her so wonderfully, his weight pressing down on her just the way she liked it.

"Ev . . ." Gasping out his name, her muscles clamped down around him as a dizzying wave of pleasure rioted through her. "My husband."

His inarticulate cry of passion was accompanied by hard, pounding thrusts that wracked her senses. Every stroke of his cock slammed deep inside of her, the delicious friction making her shudder in ecstatic passion.

It did not matter how many times they had done this in the past few weeks, this was the first time as husband and wife, and that knowledge added an extra level of excitement. Everett was hers. Truly, irrevocably, for the rest of her life, all hers.

Her climax rippled through her, a rushing wave of

rapture that drowned her in sensations. Their cries intermingled as Ev thrust hard and buried himself fully inside of her, rocking against her body, rubbing himself against her clit, and sending her past the pinnacle. It felt like she was flying as fireworks went off around her in ecstatic jubilation.

They were wrapped around each other so tightly she could not tell where she ended and Everett began . . . which was exactly how she liked it.